The Hairdryer died today

and other
Short Stories in support of the

British Deaf Association

Alison Lingwood

Contents

Foreword

Did you see *Strictly come Dancing 2021?* Wasn't it great? Which bit did you like best? The part where the music was turned off and they danced in complete silence? Who could fail to be moved?

Estimates suggest that there are over 150,000 UK users of British Sign Language, over 87,000 of whom are deaf. This figure discounts professionals working in the field.

On a more personal note, I wonder how many of us who wore masks in almost every interaction, shops, schools, transport, work environments during the Covid pandemic lockdowns, would have found it easier had we all had a basic grounding from primary school age or earlier, of BSL as a language.

Many people lose the clarity of their hearing to some degree as they get older and would benefit from this as a supplementary way of communicating.

MP Rosie Cooper tabled a Private Members Bill in June 2021 to have BSL recognised as an official language. This Bill passed unopposed through its third reading in the Commons in March and is now before the House of Lords. Is it a start? Yes, of course but it doesn't go nearly far enough.

All proceeds from *The Hairdryer died Today* will be donated to the British Deaf Association, to further their work into promotion, education and information about BSL and other ways to support the deaf community. I hope that you will enjoy the stories and spread the word to your family and friends.

To find out more about the work of the British Deaf Association contact bda@bda.org.uk or 07795 410724

20-20 Vision

'That's a lot of books. Spend your holiday
reading do you?' the shop assistant asked, ringing
their purchases through the till. Kate rather resented
this; it was no concern of the airport employee's but,
yes, they did spend a lot of time reading. Their jobs
allowed little time to relax and read anything other
than work-related documents. The airport bookstall
was an ideal place to buy books not yet available in
paperback, and anyway it was relaxing reading on the
flight and by the pool. Kate gave the assistant a tight
smile as their gate number was called.

Settling herself in her allocated seat, Kate
reached into her handbag for her reading glasses, just
as the woman in the seat in front plonked herself
down. She was a large woman – very large, and the
seat thrust backwards sharply, slamming into Kate's
reading glasses, cleanly snapping them in two across
the bridge.

Kate looked aghast at Ted. How would she

manage? A whole week being unable to read. What would she do? Ted, already secured in his seat belt merely raised his eyebrows. 'We'll buy a pair from the chemist in the local town,' was the only sympathy she got, before he returned to devouring the synopsis of his selected paperback.

'You've broke your glasses,' the little girl across the aisle whispered. Her eyes seemed to flicker around the people in the cockpit, as if afraid that she might miss something, then stared intently at Kate's face. 'I wish I could break my glasses.' Kate looked at the thick lenses the little girl had perched on her nose.

'Oh no,' she said, 'glasses are really useful. If you break them you can't see so well.'

'*You* can,' she accused. 'I saw you at the airport, you see okay without them.'

'I need mine to see little things,' Kate explained, 'and to do things like reading.'

'I can read to you if you like.' The little girl was difficult to understand over the noise of the engines and the hubbub of conversation.

'That's very kind of you, but I think I'll just save my books till I can get some new glasses. I'll watch the film instead.'

About twenty minutes into the not-very-interesting film, Kate felt a tug to her sleeve. It continued until she turned to face her little friend.

'I've drawed you a picture to cheer you up,' she whispered, her eyes searching Kate's face.

On a sheet of lined paper the little girl had captured a very fair image of a woman, recognizably Kate, looking sadly at a book with half a pair of glasses in each hand.

'That's very good,' Kate told her truthfully.

'How old are you?'

'I'm seven, nearly eight aren't I Mummy?'

The woman smiled and nodded her agreement, 'Don't bother the lady, Cara. She might want to read.'

'She can't Mummy. That lady…'

'What else can you draw, Cara?' Kate interrupted hurriedly, keen to avoid complicated explanations and the embarrassment of the glasses-wrecker, who was listening.

The little girl sucked the end of her pencil for a minute, then produced a very competent drawing of a beach with three people, obviously a child and her parents digging and sunbathing. The skill and confidence of her pencil strokes were remarkable. There was real movement to the two figures who were digging, and it was evidently a sand-castle they were building. The reclining mother-figure was lying down, not just a standing figure turned through ninety degrees. The sea looked to be shimmering as Kate squinted at it. She looked long and hard at the drawing.

Cara's eyes flickered everywhere, then rested on Kate's face, looking worried. 'Can you see it? Shall I do it bigger?' She tugged at Kate's sleeve and Kate turned and smiled at her.

'No, it's fine. It's a beautiful picture. What are you going to do with it?'

'It's for you.'

'Thank you. Do you do lots of pictures? What do you do with them?'

The girl looked tired, she had turned away and didn't hear Kate over the engine noise, so it was her turn to tug at the little girl's sleeve. She asked her question again.

'Mummy puts some on the fridge but there's such a lot of them she throws some away. I'm drawing one for your Daddy now.' Kate hid a grin as Cara indicated Ted with a wave of her pencil.

Cara's mother leaned across. 'I'd have no room in the house if I kept all her drawings.'

'She's very talented.'

Cara's mother nodded. 'She's drawn ever since she could hold a pencil, proper little drawings too, she never really went through a scribbling phase.'

Kate felt torn. She made a point of never doing business whilst on holiday, but this little lady's talent was too good to miss. She scribbled her details on a piece of paper, peering to make sure they were clear. This she handed across to Cara's mother. 'She's very young of course, but she has a real talent that should be nurtured. I am an artists' agent with a gallery in Barnes, so I sell art and represent artists.

'I have connections with collectors, the press and event organisers as well as other art professionals. The industry needs talented youngsters – these are the visual artists of the future. There are all sorts of opportunities. I'd be happy to take her under my wing. I can't promise anything of course, but she has real talent, I'd love to see how she progresses.'

Her mother looked at Kate and back at her details. Cara was busy with her drawing, but her father was leaning forward now, listening to Kate.

'That's very good of you and we live very near to Barnes, but what about Cara's disability?'

'Disability?' Kate was bemused, 'What disability?'

'Cara is deaf,' he said, 'Very soon she'll be totally deaf. She lip-reads really well and is learning

Sign Language, but...' he raised his shoulders in a gesture of frustration, 'It's an uphill struggle. So few hearing people learn Sign Language to be able to help her.'

'Perhaps,' Kate said cautiously, tapping Cara on the arm, 'we could help each other. I could help Cara with her art and she could help me to learn Sign Language.'

Their reply was lost in the announcement that passengers should fasten their seat belts. Kate was amazed, never had a journey passed so quickly.

Cara looked tired, Kate thought, it must be exhausting constantly having to be alert to signs that she would otherwise miss because she couldn't hear.

They waved goodbye and made their way to their respective hotels, having arranged to meet at Kate's gallery on a date soon after they all returned.

In the taxi, with his book finally packed away in his hand-luggage, Ted asked to see the broken glasses. 'We'll check in and then go straight to that chemist down in the town, before we even unpack. If they can't be mended they'll have some of those cheap reading glasses you can buy without prescription. '

'There's no rush,' Kate told his surprised face, 'Tomorrow will do. If I'd read throughout the journey here I'd have missed out on so much. I might just spend a bit more time this holiday looking at what's going on around me, instead of with my nose always in a book.'

Ted was bemused, 'But what about all the books you bought at the airport?'

'I'll take them home, and I'll need to find a book about Sign Language, and somewhere local that I can go and learn.

'In fact next year when we go on holiday I think might leave my reading glasses behind altogether.'

New Beginnings

In her head Tessa knew that getting another dog just now was probably not such a good idea, but once she had looked into the enclosure at the rescue centre, and her heart had seen through those limpid eyes to the little dog's soul she was doomed.

What did limpid mean anyway? She tried to distract herself, one only ever saw it written in novels, never in – say a police report or that of a solicitor, but the eyes continued to haunt her.

Knowing she was delaying the inevitable she looked back into their deep brown unblinking depths. The dog sighed and sank to her haunches, nose between her paws, and Tessa's heart was lost.

Her husband Stuart, she knew would be appalled. 'Do not come back with another dog,' he had ordered.

'Of course not, it's Ellie who wants to look for a dog, I'm just going along for moral support,' she had lied cheerfully.

Sampson, their own dog, was fourteen years

old, an elderly boy by anybody's standard, and on borrowed time for a chunky specimen of labrador.

'We'd have to do a home visit of course,' the kennel assistant told Tessa cheerfully, 'she's a sweet nature this little girl. We understand she's just turned three.' She referred to her notes, 'a Cruelty Case,' She gave it capital letters, 'she was kept in a crate 24/7 so her bum's a bit scarred. From the ammonia you know, not able to get away from her own mess.' She gave the little dog a casual rub to her head, and was licked in return.

'Just one of many to her,' Tessa muttered to Ellie, 'but to me she could be a life saver.'

If Tessa took the dog home her husband would not complain – that wasn't his way – but his face would speak volumes she knew. She suspected that he was waiting for Sampson to die. Not hoping, but waiting. Then he would be able to focus on his real passion, his garden.

There would be no more cries of, 'He's pooped on the toadflax lily again, the poor thing's choking, or plaintive moans of 'don't lift your leg on the fuchsias Sam,' whereupon Tessa would gently lead Sampson to the area they had designated the Poop Zone and which the dog had blithely ignored for fourteen years.

This morning it had been Stuart's prize acer, 'Why does he always tiddle and scratch on the most beautiful and the most expensive plants,' her husband had wailed in despair.

'Discerning – like his master?' Tessa had suggested, but this had not gone down well.

As soon as she arrived home from the kennels, she made them both a cup of tea, but now she had to own up to Stuart. Not least because the threatened home visit would take place the following day when her husband would be at home.

He took the tea from her silently and made no complaint. His expression took on that of a martyr doomed to imminent execution, but he said nothing.

'They say she's very biddable, should be easy to train,' Tessa gushed, following him into the garden, 'I'll work at it right from the start, rewards for using the Poop Zone, ignoring her for going anywhere else. And if we get her, I'll buy a lovely big pot for your acer, so big that Sam can't lift his leg on it anymore, and this little dog's a girl so your acer will be safe.'

Stuart looked underwhelmed, 'My lawn won't. I seem to remember this conversation about the Poop Zone when we got Sam fourteen years ago. It made not one scrap of difference, he always regarded the whole garden as his playground, exercise yard, loo – everything.'

Did the diminutive of the dog's name mean he was softening?

'Yes, but this time . . .' Tess never finished the promise, Stuart had given her a long look, and had then walked away.

The assessor arrived promptly next morning. She was an officious looking woman, with a tight smile, and she carried a clipboard. She explained that certain criteria would have to be met before any dog could be rehomed from the centre. They took their responsibilities very seriously. She took out her pen and began her inspection, making sure that neither Stuart nor Tessa could see what she was writing on the form.

Tom remained stoical throughout the home visit. The assessor inspected Sam's bed – newly-washed, and his water bowl, raised to accommodate his arthritis. She checked his health and immunisation records, finding them all up to date. Tess showed her the bin in which Sampson's food was stored, and the cupboard where they kept his treats. Between each, the assessor marked her form with the secretive marks. Stuart raised his eyes at Tessa, trying not to laugh. Tessa was trying not to cry.

The assessor gently examined Sam himself, checked his name tag and asked for evidence of his micro-chip. She asked a few questions about general dog-care and asked how they would manage to introduce another dog to Sam's territory. There was no way of knowing whether their answers met with her approval, but again the form was noted and the assessor asked to be shown outside.

Stuart showed her the fence that satisfactorily penned Sampson into the back garden, and the double gates with their *'Please close the gate. Dogs about'* sign. She looked around the garden, which had been swept and hosed down in preparation for this visit and another note was made. Two clean dog towels, and a cover from his bed, along with two of his tug toys were newly washed and hanging on the washing line in the sun.

The only issue arose when they viewed the Poop Zone. 'Does he use it regularly?' the stone-faced assessor asked. Resisting the temptation to ask what possible difference that could make to their suitability as dog-owners, Tessa said, 'Sometimes' in unison with her husband's emphatic 'Never.'

Raised eyebrows and a note on the pad. Tessa

followed the assessor back into the house, shouldering her husband out of the way and glaring at him to express her disapproval.

'Sorry,' he mouthed, but she feared that the damage was done.

At last the assessor reached the bottom of her form and signed it with a flourish.

For the first time she smiled, 'What will you call her? We understand that she's been known this far as Kiah K-I-A-H. It's Hawaiian apparently for *New Beginnings*.'

'That sounds a tremendous name,' her husband linked Tessa's arm and squeezed, 'New Beginnings. Very apt.'

The Hairdryer Died Today

The hairdryer died today, not with a bang or a whimper, but with that hot burning smell that you get when things attached to a plug have given up the ghost. I tried replacing the fuse but that didn't help. I asked my son-in-law to please check it over. He's an electrician you know.

His response was disheartening, 'For goodness' sake how old is it?' and then, 'It's terminal, I'm afraid. The motor's burnt out.'

Like me I thought, burnt out.

I don't know how old it is. It was my mother's originally and she died in 1979 by which time she'd already had it for a number of years. I inherited it. I don't mean literally of course as in a written item in her will, you know *To my daughter, I bequeath my hairdryer,* but more I helped myself to it when we were clearing her stuff. It was in better nick than the one at my house so we kept it and it got some heavy use throughout my daughter's teens and until she got a place of her own.

There's a sticky patch on the handle, the remains of a label. I used that hairdryer every day but couldn't on pain of death tell you the word that was written on that scrap of paper and fastened with sticky tape. I do know that it's the German word for hairdryer, and it was just one of many sticky labels posted around our home in the run-up to my daughter's GCSEs. I never learned German, but the labels must have done their stuff because she got the top grade in her German exam, and survived a year living in Austria, so it must have worked. Although I wonder how many times she was called upon to use the word 'hairdryer'. I hope the label did more for her memory than it did for mine.

That was all a very long time ago now and that label, along with all the others, is long gone. There's just this little sticky patch. I shall miss it. I'll miss having a shower, drying my hair and then having to wash my hands again to rid them of a little bit more of the remaining glue.

I've just had a look in the mirror, thinking that perhaps I don't need a hairdryer, but the hedgehog looking back at me suggests it's either buy a new one or put a paper sack over my head every time I go out, and paper sacks are getting hard to find.

*   *   *

I've been looking on the internet. There are hundreds and hundreds of hairdryers; a plethora of confusion. They all seem to be turbo-charged or super-ionic with concentrator nozzles, whatever they are. I didn't know my hair had to concentrate. I thought it just sat there.

The various offerings are mostly promoted by people I've never heard of. Perhaps I am totally out of touch or maybe these are just z-list celebrities with names and faces we're supposed to recognise and trust. Trust! That's a joke – to my mind most of them look in need of a comb, never mind a hairdryer. Are some women really seduced by this nonsense?

I don't think I've got super-ionic hair these days, if I ever did have. It's more wispy white strands with plenty of pink scalp showing through. How can a hairdryer be *Next Generation* anyway? What does that mean? The way my hair's going I'll be grateful if it manages to last out this generation.

And all these attachments! Do I want *Frizz-control* and *Volume and curls*? I thought volume was something that came on the telly. There are times when I struggle to hear that, I don't want competition from my hair. I don't like the sound either of one with *Keratin-infused ceramic.* I had to look up Keratin. The dictionary says it's a protein – the major constituent of hair: and feathers - and hoofs - and horns and claws. How does it know which I want growing out of my head?

There's one here that claims to be *Turbo-*

charged – that's positively scary. Like a rocket or a Formula One car. Mind you, it might be useful, it could probably double as a paint stripper!

And the prices! The prettiest one, that I was drawn to, is specially engineered – and engineers don't come cheap – and it features unique 3D airflow technology! 3D, that's three dimensional isn't it? I expect that means that it can dry the front of your hair at the same time as the back. The engineers may think this justifies a price-tag of over £100, I'd want it gold-plated and encrusted with diamonds for that.

I'm exhausted just thinking about all this. I think I'm going to put the kettle on now and leave the choice to my son-in-law. He'll choose the most sensible one for me – he's an electrician you know.

It's a very sad day.

The hairdryer died today.

Rupert's Story

Jenny's earliest memory of the tea trolley was of one Christmas at her grandmother's house, when it had been ceremoniously wheeled from the kitchen laden with an embroidered teacloth, patterned tea-set and post-war austerity cakes that owed more to appearance than substance.

Jenny loved the trolley; the scalloped edges and the perfect smoothness of the engine-turning, the swirly loop of the handle she loved to trace with her hand.

She had received stern lectures from her mother about acceptable behaviour when visiting Grandma and she remembered a clammy feeling to her hands when she dared that day to venture: 'What's that, Grandma?'

'That's Rupert,' Grandma answered sharply, 'We won't talk about him.'

The tone made Jenny look at Grandma's face. Her teary eyes weren't looking at the trolley at all, but beyond it at a photograph of a uniformed sailor.

Jenny knew this was of her mummy's brother, and Grandma's only son, who had been killed when the boat he was on had been sunk by Germans in something called the Atlantic.

Mummy's goodbye to the old lady seemed to Jenny to have been especially affectionate that Christmas. On the way home she had asked Mummy about the trolley, and her mother explained that it was the very last present Grandma's son Rupert had ever given to her. He had bought it especially in a fancy shop in London on his way home the Christmas before he died, so it was very special.

By the following Christmas Grandma was living in a nursing home and the Rupert trolley lived at Jenny's house. Grandma had insisted and Jenny was delighted; it was still very *à la mode,* and stood in pride of place in the corner of her mother's newly-decorated lounge. That Christmas on Rupert's lower shelf were strange exotic-looking bottles with strange exotic-sounding names like Dubonnet and Cherry B, and a row of funny-shaped glasses with yellow dancing fawns wearing blue scarves. Jenny's mother said they were champagne glasses and Jenny was very impressed. Though she never saw any champagne, that Christmas she was given a glass of Babycham to toast Grandma. *And Rupert,* Jenny added silently to herself, as the bubbles tickled her nose.

Christmases passed and fashions changed. Mini-skirts came and went; decimal money came and stayed. By the first Christmas that Jenny was married and had her own home, her mother's lounge had long been renamed *the living room* and Rupert had been relegated to the draughty hall, where he held the telephone and became a holding station for the post. As her mother's health deteriorated he also became home to an increasing layer of dust until eventually he was replaced by a modern shelf of teak.

By the time Jenny's own daughter was a teenager Rupert had been living in her mother's larder for years, where he served as additional storage for an ever-increasing supply of baking ingredients; ingredients that were seldom now used but which gathered dust and went out of date as Jenny's mother became more and more confused about what she had already bought, and about how to use the oven.

Jenny's mother died quite suddenly and she watched the family of vultures gathering as they had at her grandmother's to share out the spoils. Nobody wanted the Rupert trolley. He was no longer fashionable. Loth to part with him, Jenny put him in her garden shed along with her mother's little plastic Christmas tree, whist she considered his future. Gradually he became submerged under piles of compost, labels and plant pots, and everybody else who had known of his existence forgot that he was there.

One year in the midst of wrapping Christmas presents, Jenny suffered a stroke. The family agreed that she would have to go into a home - the very home where her grandmother had ended her days all those years before. Clearing the house, they surveyed the contents of the shed with dismay as Jenny watched through the window, but Jenny's granddaughter started pulling stuff out, piling the old wheelbarrow and the rusty lawnmower on the patio. From the back of the shed she dragged the Rupert trolley from his corner and cleared the compost and debris onto the floor with a sweep of her hand. Next she retrieved the small, plastic Christmas tree.

'It's wicked, Grandma,' she told Jenny later, running her hand over the trolley as Jenny had loved to do. 'Like, really retro. I'm going to keep it in the corner of my flat. It will be great this Christmas with the little tree on it.'

She looked puzzled, 'I'm not really sure what it is though. Would you call it a wheeled table or a dinner waggon or a tea trolley or what?'

'What would I call it?' Jenny thought for a moment, 'I think I'd just call it Rupert.'

The Non-Reader

If there is one piece of advice I would give to my younger self and to all of you, it is this: never marry a non-reader! Thankfully I never did and a real furore it caused I can tell you, calling off the nuptials at the eleventh hour as I did.

I had persuaded myself that I was *"in love"*, that this was the real thing. I completely overlooked the fact that David seemed to have few – well no – books really; mentally I stored them elsewhere, I suppose although where that elsewhere could be, I never considered.

I thought it was sweet that when we were at home together or on a train journey he would watch me read for a while, then he would gently – oh so gently – remove the book from my hands. 'There' he would say, 'now we can talk.'

And talk we did, about our pasts – mine happy and loved; his less so, and we planned for our future. We found a small flat, fairly central, that was convenient for my work and his.

We had decided not to actually move in together until our wedding night. It made it more special somehow – more significant.

The first real sign came when David called to my mother's house, where I still lived, to help me pack up stuff to move to the flat. My boss had put aside a stack of boxes for me, 'You'll need plenty,' he had said, half joking, 'for all your books if nothing else.'

When David arrived I was onto the third box, two already sealed and labelled *Books*.

'Gosh Sweetheart,' he said, 'It's only a small flat. Can't some of them stay here?'

'Not really,' I told him, 'I never know what I might want to read next, or when I might want to refer back to something or look something up.'

'But does it matter?' he looked puzzled, 'Can't you just pop round to your mum's to collect one?'

I smiled. 'What if I finished a book, say while you're watching the football, and fancied starting a specific one after we'd eaten, it wouldn't be very convenient.'

He looked genuinely taken aback, 'So, how many do you read? I thought you might read one, then go off and sort of live for a bit.' It seemed a very odd way of putting it.

Keeping my temper with difficulty I answered the first part of the question. Flipping open my diary I showed him the list. 'This month I read twelve. Of course there's been a lot to arrange for the wedding so there wasn't much spare time. Last month I read nineteen.'

David gently took the diary from my hands

and looked at the list of titles. 'Nineteen? In a single month? I see.' He flipped back a page to another list, 'What's this?'

By now I was feeling like someone with a guilty vice that I needed to be furtive about, but that was ridiculous.

'That's a list of recommendations from the Book Club and from the group that meets at the library.'

He looked genuinely shocked, 'But the Book Club, you won't carry on with that will you? Isn't it just a group of old biddies with too much time on their hands and no real life so they have to read about someone else's made-up life? I don't understand it. It's not even reading, it's just sitting around and talking about reading.'

And it was impossible to explain to a non-reader the thrill of discovering a new author, the smell of the pages, and the fun scouring internet sites and charity shops for different titles; swapping books new and second-hand with the book club, whose members drink coffee and talk about books and life. Slowly, I began to unpack the boxes.

Tonight should have been my wedding night. I don't know how David will spend it, but I shall be curled up under the duvet with a cup of hot chocolate and a good book.

Ladies who Lunch

Dora had just turned over the page on her calendar when the phone rang, which is how she knew that it was the first of August.

'Hi Mum.' It was always a pleasure to talk to Karen, her only daughter, but in the middle of Karen's working day, the call was unusual and necessarily brief.

'I know this is ridiculously early Mum, but I've booked a week's holiday starting on the twenty-third and thought we might go out for lunch on the Monday. I thought it would be a good idea to get it in the diary now, you know how other things crop up and get in the way. Are you free?'

Dora glanced at the calendar – yes that date was fine for her. They agreed that Karen and her daughter, Natalie, who would still be on holiday from school, would collect Dora late during the morning. The details could be finalised later.

The day before their planned lunch Karen called again: 'There's a slight change of plan for tomorrow, Mum. I have to call in at the Town Hall before lunch. My laptop's playing up and my week's holiday is the ideal opportunity to drop it into the IT department and let them sort it out. There is a lovely little pub across the square from the office though. That will be fine for lunch, won't it?'

Dora was happy enough. Some time to chat to Karen and Natalie would be luxury enough, they both had such busy lives.

The following morning she showered and examined the contents of her wardrobe. It was a very warm day, a coat or jacket would not be needed, so she brushed her short hair, applied the minimum of makeup and dressed in something she deemed suitable for lunch in the pub.

Karen drove Dora and Natalie into the town, arriving at about eleven o'clock. Perhaps, once Karen's work was done there would be time to look round the shops before lunch. Walking across the pedestrianised square Dora noticed a coffee shop and suggested that Natalie and she should go for a latte, Natalie's favourite, while Karen completed her business at the Town Hall.

'It should only take about twenty minutes,' Karen told her, 'There'll be somewhere for you to sit at work and I can get you both a coffee there.'

Happy to go along with the plan, Dora followed Karen and Natalie across the town. She was unfamiliar with the centre as she lived some miles away and had moved there just recently. She had heard that the Town Hall was beautiful. It would be interesting for her to visit Karen's Head Office.

Glad to get out of the sun's glare Dora followed the two of them into the cool foyer of the town hall. She had a vague impression of a couple of men hovering to the far side of the waiting area as she looked around. The first door she noticed was labelled Coroner's Officer and Dora felt slightly guilty. They had come in laughing and joking on their way to a happy lunch, and these poor men may be waiting there to register a death.

She looked over at them and did a double-take. It took a moment to absorb the fact that these two were in fact Greg, Karen's partner of four years, along with his best friend. Her daughter was speaking again as the two men came over to join them. 'Sit down Mum, and I'll tell you why you're really here.'

Dora looked stunned as Karen guided her into a chair, and stood in front of her, taking Greg's hand. 'We're getting married,' she explained, 'at quarter to twelve.'

Dora couldn't speak. She sat open-mouthed as Karen and Greg were immediately called into the Registrar's Office.

Natalie sat beside her: 'They didn't want a big fuss Gran, because they've both been married before. I kept the secret well didn't I? Even when you and I went out shopping a couple of weeks ago, and were looking in that shop window, talking about which wedding dresses we liked best – I never said a word.'

Dora hugged her, 'You did really well. I don't think I could have kept a secret like that.'

'Mum was more worried about the laptop.'

'The laptop?'

'Yes. The one she was supposed to be bringing to have mended. She was afraid you would notice that she hadn't got a laptop with her.'

Dora laughed. 'I never even thought about it.'

'Mum had to ring them up here to see if I was allowed to come, because really only the bride and groom are supposed to, with the two witnesses, and I'm not old enough to be a witness. They said that of course I could come if there was no-one to stay at home with me. They make the rule about only witnesses to stop people bringing loads of family and friends. If you want to do that they have a function room you can hire, but it costs more.'

Karen and Greg joined them again at the tail-end of the conversation.

'They'll just have to move the chairs out Mum to fit us all in. It's a tiny office. We'll have to stand up, okay?'

'If I can,' Dora smiled at her, 'I think I'm in shock.'

The wedding service was brief but lovely and in spite of having conducted hundreds, the Registrar made it special for the couple, although Dora thought that her own signature as a witness looked rather like the work of a drunken spider, her hand still shook so much.

Then came a pleasant surprise for all of them.

'The function room's not in use today,' the Registrar's clerk told them. 'I'll unlock it for you and you can take your photographs in there. There are flowers on the table. We can bring the register through and can pretend to sign it in there. It's nicer than taking photos in here or in the foyer.'

Photographs were taken on all the mobile phones the wedding group had with them, then the party left the Town Hall into the bright sunshine, to be met crossing the town square by two of Karen's colleagues laden with flowers, cards and congratulations.

In festive mood they took a table in the pub, read out the cards of good wishes and toasted the health of the bride and groom. There were presents from each of Karen's two brothers, and a number of work colleagues. It seemed to Dora that she was the only one who hadn't been let in on the secret!

Back at home, having waved goodbye to them, she put on her slippers and settled down with a cup of tea to telephone her friend Sue and recount her day's adventures.

'You'll never guess, I've just been to a wedding,' Dora told her.

'You kept that very quiet. I had no idea.' Sue sounded rather offended, until Dora explained that Karen and Jack had got married that morning and that, apart from the pub lunch, it had all been a surprise to her too.

'How exciting, and what did you wear for the wedding of the year?' Sue teased.

Dora looked down, realised what she was wearing and started to laugh, 'the bride's mother wore a pair of jeans and a t-shirt.'

The Christening Gown

It was ten years since my son's Christening and the lovely white gown he had worn was now looking a bit yellow. It was made of nylon with lace applique panels on the sleeves and skirt. The shawl, handmaid by an aunt, had washed beautifully but only made the gown look even more yellow. I liked it though, the style and shape, and my daughter would be about the same age as he was when he was Christened, so I was confident that it would fit her. I started searching the internet for how best to clean it, when a telephone call stopped all that.

My step-mother is a lovely lady. We call her Step. It began as a sort of joke, and just stuck. She was not a part of our family when my son was Christened, but had involved herself in a kind and generous way since she met and married my dad, lifting him from the depths of despair back to being a happy go lucky Dad and Grandad.

She told me that her oldest friend, Eileen, had said that she would love to make us a present of a new Christening gown if we would let her. She would smock the front and the cuffs, scallop the hem and add touches of pink for a girl.

'It would mean,' Step suggested, 'that in due course each of the children would have their own gown to use for their own children if they wanted to.'

I looked at the vaguely dingy gown hanging over the back of the chair, and agreed that it was a very kind gesture on Eileen's part. A couple of days later Step phoned to tell me how excited and privileged her friend felt to be allowed to be part of our big day, and with a toddler and a new-born I was busy enough to give it no more thought.

Until I saw Eileen's offering.

Step's face when she handed over the tissue-wrapped parcel should have told me that there was a problem, but I missed the look and enthusiastically ripped open the package.

What can I say? It was awful. The smocking was uneven, and had clearly taken several attempts. The cuffs puckered drunkenly and the scalloping around the hem was already beginning to fray. The white fabric, a cotton and polyester mixture, was also looking grubby in parts, where it had been much handled. I held it up and could see that the sleeves were stitched in unevenly, so that one was higher than the other. The baby would look like a hunchback. I didn't know what to say.

Step filled my silence, 'I know. She showed it me before wrapping it. It looks terrible, doesn't it?'

I was so upset I couldn't speak or I would have burst into tears.

'There's a note,' she said when I still hadn't said anything.

I pulled out the little card and read:

Here is the Christening gown as promised. I hope you like it. I had a bit of trouble getting the smocking right, it's a long time since I did any and I'm a bit rusty. Sadly I will be attending a Soroptomists' event in London the evening before the big day. It's a big fundraiser and, as Branch Secretary, I have to be there and so won't be able to get to the Christening ceremony. I look forward to seeing photographs though and hearing all about it.

A lifeline! Eileen wouldn't be there.

On the day of Christening our daughter was wearing the original gown, which had cleaned up really well with a little perseverance. Once we had returned to our house after the service and eaten the wonderful buffet Step had organised, the baby was stripped and redressed in Eileen's gown. She was then handed round for photographs – with her brother, with her Godparents, with us as her parents and with my dad and Step. It was a miracle of organisation and she was really getting quite cranky by the time we finished and I could put her down for a sleep.

Eileen was delighted with the photographs and nobody ever broke ranks and told her that our big grins were as a result of subterfuge to save her feelings.

Strawberry Jam and Cream

It had been a tough year and Sandra had been glad of the last of the past couple of weeks when she had at last had chance to relax.

A single mum, she had started at the local university in the same term as Carrie, her daughter, had started primary school.

When lectures permitted and in the holidays she worked as a cleaner in private houses to make ends meet. She was lucky there were so many big houses round where she lived. She could pick and choose.

And choose she did. She worked only for families with children the same sort of age as Carrie, or a little bit older. That way during the school holidays Carrie often had a playmate, or at least some age-suitable toys to play with while Sandra worked.

It was all going very well. Two of the families for whom Sandra cleaned had children in Carrie's class, and now the first university year was over, and Carrie's first parents' evening approached.

She was very excited, 'We've made a book. We all had to do a page, and then Mrs Morgan pinned them all together. I did a page about you, and Mrs Morgan says she's going to show it to you. She smiled and smiled when she read it. I think it's a nice story.'

There had been a larger than average intake to the reception class that year, and parents' evening was to be split over two consecutive evenings, alphabetically according to surname. With the surname of Walker, Sandra's appointment was for the second evening.

At eight thirty on the first of the two evenings she had a phone call from one of her employers.

'Are you going to parents' evening tomorrow, Sandra?'

'Of course, I can't wait to hear how Carrie's settled in this first year.'

'Oh, that's good. Have you had a nice couple of weeks off? You've earned it, I hope you relaxed.'

'I did. You know I love watching the tennis, that's why I always try to keep the days free during Wimbledon fortnight. I really enjoyed it.'

I could hear the smile in her voice, 'Ask Mrs Morgan about the class book if she doesn't show it you anyway. You'll enjoy what Carrie's written.'

'What …?'

'Oh, no! No spoilers. See you next week as usual.'

Arriving at the classroom door at the appointed time next evening, Sandra met another of her employers coming out of the room. 'How have you gone on with Olivia? Is she doing okay?'

Olivia's mother burst out laughing, 'Sorry, oh yes. She's doing fine.'

'What's so funny?' This was getting spooky.

'Nothing, nothing. Got to dash. See you Wednesday.'

Sandra entered the room to find several parents waiting their turn, crammed onto the tiny chairs and looking through some of their children's schoolwork. At last it was her turn for a private few minutes with the teacher. Mrs Morgan too had a wide grin.

'What's going on, Mrs Morgan? Everybody keeps grinning at me and it's making me nervous.'

'Have a look at the class book.' She pushed it over her desk so that Sandra could see it.

The children's contributions had been written a couple of days earlier, during the second week of the tennis from Wimbledon.

Carrie had written: '*My Mummy spends all day lying on the sofa, watching the telly. She drinks lots of coffee and eats scones with strawberry jam and cream. My Nanny has to come and get me from school.*'

Sandra was horrified. Without context this made her look like a terrible mother. She flushed bright red.

'Oh but ...' she began.

You don't need to explain.' The teacher was still smiling.

'Oh, but I do, you see . . .'

Mrs Morgan placed her hand on Sandra's arm. 'No, really. At least four people have told me how hard you work; bringing Carrie up on your own; working hours that fit in with her and your mum's commitments, and studying for your degree. I commend you, I really do. You're doing a great job with Carrie. Her reading and writing are well on target for her age, and her number work is very advanced.'

Sandra was stunned. 'Thank you.'

Mrs Morgan smiled warmly and Sandra knew that she and Carrie were doing just fine.

'We all deserve our holidays. I know I'm glad enough for mine, and anyway it could be a lot worse.'

'How is that?'

'Carrie came to ask for my help because she didn't know how to spell coffee. Just think – it could have been gin.'

Grandad Tick Tock

I want to tell you firstly a bit about my family. When I was growing up it seemed that other people always had interesting stories to tell about their families, adventures even, but I had nothing to offer. My mum married my dad Phillip about a hundred years ago, and in due course had my brother Simon and then me. My brother had, according to my parents, flown the nest and now I feel they are waiting for me to do the same.

See what I mean? Not very interesting is it? At least it wasn't until out of the blue an airmail letter arrived from Australia.

The letter was addressed solely to my dad, which was unusual in itself. He read it in silence, then handed it to Mum, who read it, said 'What the ...?' and passed it to me. This is how it read:

Dear Phillip,

I think this letter will come as a massive surprise – I hope a pleasant one, although I may be wrong and you may already know all about me. My name is Audrey Satchwell and I believe I'm your sister – well, your half-sister to be strictly correct.

At Christmas I was given one of these Find your Ancestors kits. I don't know about in the UK but here in Australia they are all the rage just now, as well as a whole raft of television shows. Anyhow, I did the test and it came back as a match with someone called Simon, who I think might be your son. The connection is close enough to be a cousin, or a sibling's son, and his DNA was on the database. (I may be wrong with all this of course, but I don't think I am.)

To help you I'll give you some information about my dad – who I think is your dad too. He worked as an engineer and came from a quite well-to-do family who lived in a big house. I looked on Google and the house seems to be quite near to where you live now. I looked up your local phone directory and there was only one person with your surname. It's not that common a name - or it isn't here anyway - so I took a punt on you being the right person. If you're not, perhaps you'll be able to put me in touch with the brother I'm looking for.

Anyhow my mother was Amy and she

worked as a sort of housemaid or live-in help at the home where your dad was brought up. Your Great-Gran was alive then and part of my mam's job was looking after the old lady who never came downstairs. Mam must have been about fifteen or so, and your dad was a lot older. He was married already. Anyhow nature took its course you might say and before long my mam found she was expecting me.

By the time I was born your mam was expecting a baby herself – that would be you, Phillip. My mam was very quickly married off to a man in the town and they were set up in a little cottage that your dad's family owned. Then in the seventies they took advantage of the Ten Pound Poms scheme to come over here. I remember though, long before that, a man who came to visit us and he had a boy on the back of his motorbike. I think that boy may have been you.

Anyway, that's enough for now. I'd love for you to get in touch if you think I might be right, and if not, then I'm sorry for wasting your time. I do hope I hear from you soon.

Audrey Satchwell

'Grandad Tick Tock!' I said.

Both my grandfathers had been alive when I was small, although sadly no longer, and Simon and I made the distinction between the two by means of this nickname, though his real name was Robert or Bob. Even my mum and dad called him Grandad Tick Tock. He always looked very dapper, wore a three piece suit with a bow tie, and had shoes polished to a mirror-like shine. He had a shock of white hair, smoothed down with some sort of hair product and a neat little moustache. Across the waistcoat of his suit he always wore a gold pocket watch, which he would hold up to our ears so we could hear it ticking.

'I know Simon got one of those DNA kits,' my mum said, 'he said that it could be a laugh. Do you think she's right Phillip?'

My dad looked stunned. 'I remember,' he said, 'I remember going with my dad on the back of his motorbike to visit some people who lived on the other side of town. My dad said that they were family friends, but Mum didn't like them much so it could be just somewhere we went for a day out on the bike. I was to call her Aunty Amy and I can't remember his name. He was usually out at work I suppose, but there was a girl a bit older than me. We would play in the garden if it was nice while the grown-ups talked. That must have been this Audrey woman. And another thing, the *Old Lady* she talks about, the one who never came downstairs? That would be my great-grandmother and her name was Audrey too. Amy must have named her little girl after the old lady. One time I remember Grandad Tick Tock giving Aunty Amy some money just before we left. I asked him about it and he said he owed it to her. I never thought to question why. How extraordinary, I haven't thought about that for years.'

'If you remember it Dad, and you were taken on the back of the motorbike, how old were you?'

He thought for a while, 'I must have been about nine or ten. Dad didn't let me go on the bike till that sort of age. Presumably before that he went to see them on his own,' he shrugged.

My mum was stunned, 'So he hadn't abandoned Amy. Grandad Tick Tock'd made sure she was all right all that time, and presumably paid her too. Wow!'

*   *   *

Letters and copies of photographs passed back and forth until the one where Audrey said that she and her husband Eric would be visiting the UK and would love to visit. They would stay in a local hotel over two nights if that suited Phillip.

After the visit another photograph joined those framed and displayed on my mum's sideboard, one of Phillip and Audrey side by side on the sofa. The likeness was startling. My dad said that his only regret was that Grandad Tick Tock was long dead. He would have loved to show the photo to the old man, and to learn more about his second family. He would have liked too, to let him know that he bore no grudges about his past, and was delighted that he had found his sister Audrey.

Covid hit the world wreaking devastation, and even more draconian measures were introduced in Australia than in the UK. For a long time communication was sparse. My dad was hesitant to write, not knowing whether Audrey and Eric had been hit by the virus. He guessed that they probably felt the same about him.

Eventually a letter arrived, but in a different handwriting. This was from Eric, saying that Audrey had sadly passed away the previous year. She had suffered from cancer once before, and it had returned, but this time there had been no reprieve. He wanted her brother to know how much happiness it had brought to Audrey to find him again, and to tell him that she had had a copy of the photograph of the two of them next to her hospital bed right till the end. He said he was sending a parcel that might interest Phillip and Simon, whose DNA search had started it all.

Four weeks later the small parcel arrived from Australia. It took my dad ages to open it, it was so well packaged. Eventually he tore off the last layer of protection and sat looking at the contents for a long time before he spoke. The parcel contained a small flattish box and a note, much crumpled and very grubby, obviously folded and refolded often, as if it had been read and reread over many years. My dad peered at it to make out the faded writing, then he shook his head and it was a while before he spoke.

At last he seemed to pull himself together, 'I always wondered,' he said. 'When Grandad Tick Tock died my mum cleared everything of his out, threw stuff away. I don't know what happened to most of it, but listen to this:

To my dearest girl,
I'm sending you my gold pocket watch my dear Amy. It might be worth a bit of money. If ever you get short you can always sell it. Otherwise you can keep it as a reminder of our happy times together.
With love always, your Bob

There's no date, but this must have been written shortly before he died. So all that time he must have known exactly where she was.'

There nestled in a protective bed of cotton wool, ticking away quietly, as it had always done, was Grandad Tick Tock's gold pocket watch.

Rear Window

It had been one of those days. Donna's daughter had knocked over a bottle of milk at the breakfast table, meaning that not only was there no cereal and just black coffee for her to start the day, but also that a thorough cleaning job would be facing her later.

She had dashed to visit her mum who had been unwell and, seeing the older lady through the kitchen window on her approach, noticed how old and frail she was looking. Donna wondered how much longer she was going to be able to go on living on her own.

Now as she swung right at the mini roundabout she became aware of the two cars immediately behind her. The one looming in her rear-view mirror was a large silver SUV that seemed thoroughly out of place in the suburbs, but what really caught her attention was that the woman driving the car was evidently in a hurry; a very great, impatient hurry. As Donna drove between the two rows of social housing, the woman was gesticulating and obviously looking for an opportunity to overtake. There was no such opportunity. These houses had no drives, and so there were vehicles parked along either side, half on the footpath, as the road narrowed towards a bridge. This bridge was wide enough to accommodate only one vehicle, and so was controlled with traffic lights. As Donna approached, the lights changed to amber and she slowed to a stop as they turned red.

This gave her the chance now to look back more closely at the SUV driver, who seemed incandescent. She was banging on the steering wheel, and mouthing something which Donna guessed were not terms of endearment. At first she thought the woman might be carrying on an irate phone call on a hands-free unit but no, the display of histrionics seemed to be for her benefit. Donna was quite surprised. Presumably this woman was annoyed that she had obeyed the Highway Code and the law, by stopping at a red light.

As the lights changed and Donna moved off the woman pulled as close in behind her as she could. It occurred to Donna that she had only to just flip the brake pedal and the woman would drive into the back of her car. It was tempting, the fallout would almost be worth it, but she really didn't have time for all that today. She took off, sticking to the thirty miles an hour limit, oncoming traffic again thwarting the woman's attempts to overtake. Several times as Donna glanced in the mirror she noticed the woman waving her arms about, obviously with no control of the car at all.

A hundred yards or so beyond the bridge was the first of a series of speed bumps. The road passed between the sixth form college on the left, and the Fire Station on the right. There were two sets of traffic lights, one to allow the emergency services egress from the fire station, and the second set pedestrian lights directly opposite the college. Of course at this time in the morning the button on the pedestrian lights was being repeatedly pressed by students, plus there was a constant stream of youngsters straggling across the road wherever they felt like it.

These speed bumps, of which there were eight in total, were absolutely vicious. They had to be taken at no more than ten miles an hour if you wanted to continue with your car's underparts intact. Throughout the whole of this part of the journey the woman in the car behind kept gesticulating, occasionally hitting her horn – it was getting ruder now – and mouthing at Donna, who was starting to find it all rather funny.

Beyond the speed bumps the road eventually widened into three lanes just before it met the roundabout where it crossed a more major road. The left hand lane was marked with the arrow indicating Turn Left Only. The central lane had a straight arrow indicating straight ahead only, and the right hand lane had a dual arrow indicating the acceptability of going straight across the roundabout or turning right. Two lanes allowing traffic to go straight across the roundabout was logical, as there was a short span of dual carriageway opposite, hence two lanes fed into two lanes.

The road leaving the roundabout directly opposite Donna's approach was the route she planned to take. With two potential lanes to choose from she went for the middle lane. Several cars and the college bus were on the outside lane indicating to turn right.

Do you believe in a sixth sense? Donna just suddenly intuited that her impatient follower, who had taken the inside lane, had no intention at all of turning left onto the main road as prescribed by the lane markings, but every intention of undertaking her on the roundabout and cutting in. This is exactly what happened.

You will be wondering why I mentioned right at the beginning of this little tale, that two cars had pulled out behind Donna as she first left that mini roundabout now a couple of miles behind her. What had very quickly become evident to Donna was that the irate woman in the SUV had not looked in her rear view mirror since that point, otherwise she would have been aware that the car immediately behind her was a marked police car.

As Donna drove off up the dual carriageway, a last glance in her own mirror showed quite clearly the police officer, who had flagged down the irate SUV driver, getting out of his own and putting his hat on as he approached her car.

He had seen it all, and Donna reflected that karma could indeed be very sweet.

Keys in the Fruit Bowl

I'm Pat and my husband of fourteen years is Terry. Prosaic-sounding names aren't they? But they suit us. Our life was jogging along very comfortably, or so I thought. We both had good jobs and we had two children who seemed to be a lot less trouble than many. We had recently moved into a larger detached house on a nice estate and that was when things changed.

I had dressed up for this party. The dress, not new but never worn round here before, was a bit dowdy but a gold necklace brightened it up. As I plonked down in front of the dressing table to do my make-up, the velvet padded seat gave a deep sigh. I had put on a bit of weight over the years, and some of the cosmetics I dug out of the drawer were rather ancient as I seldom bothered.

I'd come home from work one day last week to find Terry quite excited. He had met the woman who lived about five doors down, the house with pampas grass in the front garden he explained, and she had invited them to the get-together that evening. That was how she referred to it, a get-together.

'She seems very friendly. It'll be a chance to meet the neighbours,' Terry enthused, 'Parents of potential friends for the children, it'll be great. She said there'll be about eight other couples there.'

I had to agree it would be nice to put names to a few of the faces I had seen around. There were no immediately local shops, so everyone on the road seemed to jump in their car and head to the nearest supermarket. Until school started in September there would be no clubs for the children to join. It would be good for them to get to know some families who were at the same school.

And so, leaving the children with my mum, here we were, me perched awkwardly on a squashy sofa in front of the coffee table and Terry talking to Kyra, who I had immediately thought of as our tarty hostess. Kyra wore a blood red dress. Her matching lipstick dominated over-heavy makeup and the bling dangling from her wrists was overdone for my taste.

When we arrived Kyra had instructed Terry to just *Chuck his keys on the table,* as she took our coats. After a quick introduction of names, so fast that they were immediately forgotten, I noticed that Terry's keys were now in the fruit bowl on the table, along with several other sets of keys.

Standing fairly close to me was a quiet man who was, if not exactly uncomfortable, then simply resigned to the proceedings as other people milled around and chatted. This was not the introduction to the neighbours I had expected, and I had no intention of staying long. I tried to catch Terry's eye, but he was evidently enjoying himself talking to Kyra, who was a very touchy-feely person, too much so in my opinion, touching the front of his shirt with her bright red talons as she spoke to him and laughing over-loudly at everything he said. She was so obvious, but Terry seemed to be lapping it up. I shrank further and further into the corner of the sofa, eyeing the bowl of keys as if they might burn me, as indeed they might.

The quiet man glanced at his watch and sighed quietly to himself. I caught his eye, 'You don't look totally happy to be a part of all this,' he said, sitting on the adjacent chair.

'I'm not,' I admitted, 'I had no idea when Terry said we'd been invited to a little party to meet some of the neighbours that this was what he meant,' I nodded at the bowl, 'He must have had an idea though, been told something. Do you come to many of these?'

'Oh yes,' he said bitterly, 'All of them. Is that your husband talking to ...'

'Yes, that's my husband, making an exhibition of himself.' I watched as Terry swayed closer to Kyra as he half-crooned, half croaked *Lady in Red* in her ear.

'I was going to ask you about the tart in the red dress, but that's unkind. I don't know her and yet I'm judging her. She probably would refer to me as the *Frump in Blue.*'

'Not unkind at all,' he said, 'I'm Alastair by the way.' He shook hands with me awkwardly without getting up, and I found myself smiling for the first time all evening. 'Are you here on your own?' I was puzzled. Couples had drifted out of the room, there had been the sound of the front door closing and cars driving away. In the fruit bowl just one set of keys remained –Terry's.

'You could say that,' he said ruefully, 'the tart in red is my wife.'

'Oh, I'm sorry. I didn't mean to …'

He shook his head, 'You've only just met her and you've summed her up beautifully. Every six weeks or so she gets bored of her current squeeze, holds one of these parties and picks someone else. Shall we get out of here?'

We walked down the road in silence, I had I hoped made it quite clear that I wasn't interested in the whole wife-swapping thing, even if Terry seemed keen, but I was secretly fearful of what Alastair had in mind. In fact all he wanted of me was a cup of coffee and a chat. He told me he only stayed with Kyra for the sake of his children. Whatever affection there had been was well and truly obliterated by this apparent need of hers to sleep with other people. I put off talking about my relationship with Terry, which I had thought of as okay, not sparkling but after fourteen years who would realistically have expected that?

Terry and I never got to celebrate fifteen years of marriage. He was besotted with Kyra and returned home the following lunchtime only long enough to pack a bag. He promised to keep paying for the house, visit the children all the time and finished by asking where Alastair was.

'At the guest house down the road I believe. He said that this happens on a fairly regular basis when his wife gets bored. You are being played for a fool.'

'You don't understand,' he told me.

'I think I understand a lot more than you do, but' I looked at the bag, 'if you're determined to be made a fool of I can't stop you.'

We would have been married for fifteen years today, if the marriage had lasted that long; if he had not become besotted with Kyra; if she had not thrown him out after six weeks as Alastair had foretold; if I had agreed to his pleas to come back to us, instead of telling him that his children had been crying for him for six weeks, and were just beginning to get over it.

Alastair had moved out of the local hotel where he had been staying and was now living back with Kyra, ignoring the situation with Terry as he had done all the other times.

And what became of my ex-husband? Terry eventually realised how he thrown away everything he cared about, losing his wife, his children and his home all for a brief bit of fun. He hanged himself from a beam in the warehouse where he worked, and neither Kyra nor Alastair even bothered to attend his funeral.

Skipjack

I've been known as Skipjack for nearly as long as I can remember. My real name is John Taylor, but Skipjack sounds more interesting and suits me much better.

It started when I was at primary school. There was very little money in our house, five kids and a dad who hadn't worked since he fell off his window cleaning ladder years before. I don't even remember the accident happening, it was so long ago and my mam used to keep us all by going out cleaning in the mornings, and pulling pints in the Jolly Roger every evening.

Well it wasn't every evening of course, Sundays the pub was shut and even sitting at home my mam and dad would get dressed up in their best clothes. For my dad that was a suit of course, but on Sundays he wore a shirt and tie with it too. My mam would wear a blouse with her *best* skirt, although that skirt had darns in it if you looked closely.

My mam and dad share the same birthday! I know, how weird is that? Everybody seems really surprised when we tell them, so I guess it must be pretty unusual. I wanted to get them a nice present, but I had no money to get them anything at all – I must have been about nine or ten and wasn't even old enough to have a paper round.

Then I was walking to school one day past one of the big houses along the way and they had workmen there, and a giant skip on the drive.

One of the workmen was putting an empty pallet onto the skip, when I called out to stop him. I still don't really know why, except that the wood looked a lovely colour in the morning sun and it seemed so sad to just throw it into a skip to be buried in other rubbish.

'Can I have it?' I asked, 'Please.'

'You can lad, yeah. Whatya gonna do with it?'

'I don't know. Make something for my mam and dad. It's their birthday soon.'

'What's your name, lad?'

'John Taylor, but everyone calls me Jack.'

'Hiya Jack. I'm Todd. Tell you what, let me know where you live, I'll break the pallet up into planks and drop it off for you.'

I was a bit worried. 'I'm not really supposed to talk to strange men.'

'Well, that's very sensible but you've already done that haven't you? Too late now.' He cracked a huge toothy grin. 'Say, have you got a back way into your garden or somewhere I can drop the wood off, then it won't spoil the surprise for your mam and dad?

I thought about it. I'd already spoken to him now hadn't I and broken my mam and dad's rules. I smiled and thanked him very much.

'We haven't got a garden, but there's an alley at the back of the yard. Nobody goes out there till bin day next week.'

'The alleyway it is then. It won't be till late mind, on my way home from work.'

'That's okay. Thank you for doing it for me.' I bit my lip, 'I'm not sure what I'm going to do with it.' Suddenly the idea didn't seem such a good one.

'Tell you what,' Todd said, 'I'll put my thinking cap on too and see if I can come up with any ideas.'

School took forever that day, and it was a long day 'cos I had extra English after school. That's 'cos I'm not very good at writing and that and am getting help from my teacher. I don't think it's working that well though. However hard I try the letters and words just won't sort themselves out. That day I had to write the start of a story, so I wrote:

A man gav me some woud tody and
I'm make my mam a present. I don't no
yet what to make

I gave my work in at the end of the session and listened miserably while the teacher talked me through the mistakes. He didn't put it like that of course, he would say that he was pointing out how my work could be made better, which basically amounted to stop making mistakes.

He talked a bit about the work I had done, then asked me about the present I was making. I told him I didn't know yet, but I'd got some wood out of a skip.

'Skipjack,' he said, 'that's a sort of fish, a

tuna.' I nodded, we ate a lot of tuna in our house, it's cheap. 'But it's also a pun. Do you know what a pun is?' I shook my head.

'It's when you play around with words to make a joke. Jack, that's you, getting wood out of a skip, put them together makes Skipjack.' He could see I was losing interest, but I smiled obligingly, 'that's funny sir.'

He said that if I wanted any varnish for my wood he had some left over from something he had made in his kitchen. I said thank you, but I was more interested in getting home to look at the wood, if Todd had actually left it of course.

He had. There behind our broken down back gate was a pile of lovely clean slats from the pallet. He'd taken all the nails out and everything, and I think it was smoother like he'd rubbed it down a bit. There was loads of it. Stuck to the top with some sort of tape was a sandwich bag. The writing on the bag was even worse than mine, but I suppose in his job Todd didn't have to write much stuff down. The bag had some nails inside it, bright new shiny nails, which was really thoughtful of him, I hadn't thought about how I was going to fix it together. It took me ages to read the note, but eventually I got it. He wanted to see me the next day. He had an idea for my present.

There was no sign of Todd when I walked past the big house next morning, just a grumpy looking old man. I wondered whether the wood and nails really belonged to him and I hurried past with my head down. I was unhappy not to see Todd but when I got to school I found a part tin of varnish, and even a brush in my desk. Another note – I was having to read a lot lately. This one read: *I thought this might be useful Skipjack. Keep the brush. I won't need it again. I'd love to see your present when you've finished it.*

After school I hurried on my way, clutching the tin of varnish, wondering how I was going to sneak it indoors when I got home. As I walked past the big house I heard a shout: 'Oi, Jack,' and Todd was hurrying down the path, 'Did you find it? I was worried it might get nicked, it's a bit rough round there innit?'

I supposed he was right, but I'd never thought about it. To me it was just home.

'It's there,' I said, 'Thank you.' I went to walk on, but he hadn't finished yet, 'Hang on. I've got summat else for you.'

I followed him partway up the drive, but the house was massive and I didn't want to see either the owners or the grumpy guy who I took to be Todd's boss so I lagged behind.

He came back to me after a few minutes with a folded piece of newspaper and a piece of rope.

'Thanks for the nails,' I said, then parroting adults I had heard, 'what do I owe you?'

'Nowt,' he winked and looked around, 'there's always nails and stuff lying about. Don't worry about it. Now, this 'ere is a bit of a pattern.' He showed me an outline in pen that was drawn onto the newspaper. 'If you can cut that shape out then drill a hole here,' he indicated where he had put a cross, 'then put this rope through the hole and you can hang it up. See? The shape of it means that there are these slots to hook plant pots into, just ordinary little pots, nowt special. Then your mam can grow seeds in it and stuff.' I remember he gave me a big grin, as if he was pleased to be part of the enterprise.

I told him about the varnish from the teacher, and about the nickname Skipjack. He must have understood the pun without me explaining, because he laughed out loud. 'That's brilliant, that is. He must be a right clever bloke your teacher.'

'I think he is, loads cleverer than me any'ow.'

There was a shout from the side of the house and Grumpy Face appeared. Todd gave me another wink, 'Gotta go. Good luck Skipjack.'

'Thanks Todd.' I was aware that I sounded less than enthusiastic. My mind was rushing around how on earth I could get hold of a saw to make the shape, a drill to make the hole, and as for soil and plant pots and seeds I had no idea. I'd been thinking perhaps about a little shelf for in the kitchen or something, but this plant thingy sounded lovely. If only …

Next day in school my teacher must have seen that I was fed-up and took me to one side at break time. I told him all about it. I normally keep things to myself, but I found myself pouring out the whole story. That I had come so far but that the end seemed unachievable.

After a few minutes he asked what I did at the weekends. I told him there was nothing special. With all of us at home in our little house and Mam trying to do the washing and everything it got a bit crowded, so I would take any chance to get out. He suggested I call round with my piece of wood, the pattern and the rope and he would see if he could help.

By the end of that Saturday we had made a plant holder. My teacher had helped me with the sawing and the drilling. We'd rubbed down and varnished the piece of pallet board and then he'd found three little plant pots and showed me how to fill them from a bag of compost. Then we went out into his own back garden with a trowel and dug up three little pansies, and he showed me how to plant them up.

The most special part of that day was something I hadn't even thought about.

'Keep the pattern,' he told me as I was about to tear it up. 'Patterns can always be reused. I'll tell you what – I know someone who would like one of those plant pot hangers. If you come around again, you can borrow my tools. It'll be good practice for you, then when it's finished I'll buy the plant pot holder off you for my friend.

'You've got enough rope for a second one and enough varnish. Then with the money from selling that you can buy some more rope and another tin of varnish and so on. That's how businesses start, Skipjack. You could make more of those and sell them.'

When the birthday came around my mam and dad were delighted with the little plant pot holder, and hung it in our little yard. That was the start of it. I'd already sold one to my teacher, and another teacher wanted me to make two for him.

*   *   *

I'm going to fast forward now to today. I have a successful business and live in a house as big as that one that Todd worked at. I have an arrangement with the council that I can clear stuff I can use that's been fly-tipped, or where householders have asked them how to dispose of useful stuff. For the most part it's a happy arrangement. Of course I couldn't use all the stuff and I've a yard at the back, a Reclamation Yard they call it, but I employ my brother to run that for the most part. My sister works there too, she's good on the numbers and writing and that. That way I can do what I really love, which is making things from wood. I'm not much into reading and writing even now, but it doesn't seem to matter so much anymore.

I still keep an eye out for Todd on my travels, but I've never seen him again. I wonder sometimes whether he ever sees the name of my business and remembers. I've called the business *Skipjack's* to make sure I never forget that young lad, who can still barely write, and that very first pallet that they rescued together.

Nine Double Decker Buses

Passengers in my car often comment about the distance I leave between my bonnet and the vehicle in front. Other drivers must feel it excessive too as they often seem to take it as permission to nip in between the two. I've got used to this now and it no longer annoys me, I just drop back with a smile to myself and let them get on with it.

It all goes back to my final driving lesson. I had passed my Theory Test what seemed like ages ago, but the Covid outbreak interrupted my regular lessons, and I was getting very close to the two year cut-off point, after which I would have had to take my Theory Test again.

'There are no exceptions to this rule,' I had read in the relevant information. It didn't seem quite fair, but I suppose it wouldn't be safe to let people like me on the road when we hadn't had any practice in more than two years. So I saved my money and splashed out on another half dozen lessons. I could not afford to fail.

We're very lucky round here in that we have a short stretch of dual carriageway that is the nearest thing to driving on a motorway that a learner is allowed to do, and at some times of the day there is a parade of L plates driving in each direction along this road, taking advantage of the opportunity to be allowed to travel at up to seventy miles an hour.

I was taking my last, or what I hoped would be my last, driving lesson; the one where your hour-long slot ends up not back at home but at the Test Centre.

There were so many people looking to book their tests now that Lockdown had ended, that the time slots had filled up really quickly, and my slot had been fixed for the evening. Being summer it was daylight, and being after seven o'clock the traffic would have calmed down from its inevitable commuter rush.

As I was steadily driving along during this lesson, careful not to exceed the seventy mph limit, the driving instructor said, 'You're doing very well, my dear,' He always called me 'my dear.' I suppose he saw so many people in a day it was easier than checking his notes for a name each time. I wonder what he used to call the men he taught. 'You're doing very well, my dear, but I'd like you to drop back a bit further from the car in front. You need to give that driver enough space to do something stupid.'

When we reached the Test Centre we had a few moments to wait and I think he had planned that we arrived a little early. He consulted the Highway Code and let me have a look at the relevant section. *'The stopping distance for a vehicle travelling at seventy miles per hour is 96 metres,'* I read, 'Why they can't standardise these measurements, either go Imperial or metric, but a mixture of the two makes no sense.'

'Ninety six metres,' he explained 'is the equivalent of over nine double decker buses nose to tail.'

That shut me up.

'That's how far back you need to be when you're on a dual carriageway or a motorway and conditions are favourable. That means when it's daylight, clear and dry. Otherwise your stopping time can be much more, sometimes as much as double. The vast majority of drivers on the motorway travel at or around the speed limit, so you need to bear this in mind whenever you get behind the wheel. Now in you go, and very good luck.'

The test seemed to go well. We were on our way back to the test centre along the dual carriageway. I was feeling a bit of a fool, I had twice dropped back because cars had ducked in between me and the vehicle I was following and I was thinking to myself that this surely wasn't how it was in real life, and then it happened.

At this point the road went through a cutting with steep banks shelving up on either side. Suddenly the car in front of me, for no apparent reason, veered to the left, and up the embankment. It seemed to hang there for a moment, then the momentum flipped the front end over and it landed on its roof, directly in front of me. 'Very good emergency stop,' the tester said, then, 'Are you okay? Sit here while I go and check.'

I couldn't have gone with him, my legs had gone to jelly. We were barely half a mile away from where my instructor had first mentioned that I was driving too close, little more than an hour ago. If I had been driving as I was then, that car would have come down either immediately in front of us and I would have driven into it, or it would have landed on top of us. Either way it would have been carnage.

I watched as two youths, obviously the worse for drink, climbed out of the front windows of the vehicle, laughing and apparently unharmed.

Someone in the queue that was building up behind us had phoned the police. We waited long enough for them to arrive and give them our details, then were allowed on our way.

'I've passed,' I said jubilantly to my instructor who had been anxiously waiting.

'You were out longer than normal,' he said, 'I thought something terrible might have happened.'

'If it hadn't been for you,' I told him, 'it would have done.'

The Ricardian Lie

To: drunkellie@internet.com June 1st

I did it Ellie. It was an absolute fluke, but I got to go to Shakespeare's Globe on the South Bank at last. Dan had told me that he would be away over my birthday weekend in Surrey for a conference. I made a bit of a fuss although it wasn't his fault, and he suggested that I go along with him and he would get me a ticket to see a show of some sort if I didn't mind going into the city on my own. You know I've always wanted to visit Shakespeare's Globe from the time we were at school. Not the original one of course, that burnt down in 1613, but the new one on London's South Bank, as close to the original as Health and Safety restrictions would allow. Sorry, you probably know all this. Anyway, the theatre didn't disappoint.

We had a look on line and Twelfth Night was opening on the Sunday with Fancy Dewar, that comedian playing Malvolio and there was a matinee, but when I told Dan he said even the matinee would mean him driving home too late on the Sunday when we both had to get up for work the next morning. So the Saturday matinee it had to be.

So, when I achieved my ambition that Saturday afternoon the wonderful Trevor P Hughes was playing Richard III. He was marvellous, bringing real pathos to Shakespeare's lies, despite his own personal convictions that much of 'Shakespeare' was not written by Shakespeare at all.

To: blooRuby@internet.com June 2nd
Ruby, I'm so glad you got your wish, although it seems a weird play to choose. Could you not have waited for a comedy another time and gone together with Dan? Sorry, there I go as usual, telling my married friends how to live their lives. I was surprised though when you chose that play. Wasn't he a total monster, killing those poor little princes in the tower and all? Even I remember that story and he was awful. You've got me interested now, but I don't know much about it.

To: drunkellie@internet.com June 2nd
I remember you were never really into history at school, gave it up in favour of science didn't you at the end of Year 9? I can give you some background, but I warn you it does get complicated. And no, I'm not being patronising or suggesting you won't understand it. The first thing you have to remember is that history is always written by the winning side in any conflict.

To: blooRuby@internet.com June 2nd
I know, I know, but I was right wasn't I to

concentrate on science? I've made a career of it, I could certainly couldn't have done that about history. The main thing I remember is that there was lots of infighting; strong, wealthy families calling the tune if they spotted any chink in the armour (no pun intended) of the royals.

To: drunkellie@internet.com June 2nd
That sums it up very nicely, Ellie. I'll try to keep it simple, because there were lots of twists and turns – I think that's what I find interesting. I suppose it's like the equivalent of your excitement at what you find in your Petri dish or whatever.

There are two main families who play a major part and already it gets difficult to simplify. The Plantagenets have been on the throne since 1216. It hasn't been a peaceful time, the Plantagenets were Lancastrians and Yorkists, and you'll remember the War of the Roses – hearing of it at least. It went on for years and years. Richard III had an older brother who became Edward IV, and he was the eldest child of several. Next in line was George, then Edmund (forget him, he doesn't play much of a part), then Richard. There were others but I'm trying to keep it straightforward.

The other significant family member is their sister Elizabeth. I'm going to call her Young Elizabeth, because they seemed to have no imagination in those days and gave their kids their own names. The mother of all these offspring was Elizabeth Woodville. Are you with me so far?

To: blooRuby@internet.com June 3rd
I don't remember you being this patronising at

school, Ruby, lol. What about these two powerful families then, who were they?

To: drunkellie@internet.com June 4th
    The two families with most power, wealth and ambition at the time were the Nevilles and the Woodvilles. It was in their interests to be on the winning side of any battles.
    Firstly, the Nevill family. Richard Nevill was called the Kingmaker, and played a big part in helping Edward IV, (Richard's oldest brother) who was only 19 when he was crowned, in the early stages.
    Then there's the Woodville family. Edward IV's mother was a Woodville, and we can't underestimate how strong and feisty a woman she was, just like the rest of her family. (Incidentally, Edward IV and Richard III's sister, young Elizabeth, went on to marry Henry VII.)
    I'd ask if you're still with me, but I don't want to seem patronising, lol. You may want to flip back as the story unfolds.

To: blooRuby@internet.com June 4th
    Blimey! Has the story not started yet? We're two days into this exchange, I've had about a million emails from you and already my brain hurts. Okay – rant over – carry on. I know Henry VII was the first Tudor king and that he followed on immediately after Richard III. You still haven't explained about how and why the monster Richard murdered those little boys.

To: drunkellie@internet.com June 4th
    Ellie! You have fallen victim to Shakespeare's

hype. Richard wasn't a monster at all. He did all sorts of good things. He was beloved in Ireland and across the north of England and these were the people who knew him best. He was a fearsome warrior, and yet spared a few people who, the future showed, he would have been better off without. He loved those two boys. He continued to employ Young Edward's tutor and entourage after the death of his father Edward IV, had a requiem mass for his brother held at York, bought them clothes even, in preparation for Young Edward's coronation in due course.

There were the two other brothers between the Edward IV and Richard in age, yet it was Richard, who was still a teenager, who Edward chose to make guardian of his sons, and when the time came, Protector of the Realm. He really was very popular during his lifetime and really wanted to heal the country. He was well liked and devoted to his wife and young son. He was totally devastated when first the little boy, and then his wife died within a year of each other. Most importantly, there was no suggestion that he had anything against the young princes.

To: blooRuby@internet.com June 5th

Okay, okay so he wasn't all bad, nobody is all bad, but how can you say he had nothing against the boys when they were imprisoned in the Tower of London? That's definite isn't it? That's not made up.

Then on that first email you mentioned *Shakespeare's lies*. Shakespeare was a serious playwright you know, thought to have a great deal of gravitas in his day. Even the members of the royal family were big fans.

To:

Okay. At that time the Tower of London was one of the royal residences, it was a palace not a prison. Later it was used differently, because it was so close to the Thames it was easy to defend, but that was exactly why it was built there in the first place. The princes lived there, they weren't captive. Anyway a lot of Young Edward's education took place at another royal residence, Ludlow Castle. The boys weren't at the Tower all the time.

As for Shakespeare's version of the story, of course it was all lies, Ellie. The grotesque-looking hunchback of Shakespeare's play in fact suffered from mild scoliosis of the spine. That was demonstrated when his remains were found under that Leicester car park. So I need to get my thoughts together.

To answer your point about Shakespeare's writing impressing the Royal Family, I can only say that today he would probably be called a *Grifter*. Don't think I have a down on the guy – I love Shakespeare's plays, but he had two households, one in Stratford, one in London and a whole company of actors, all relying on him to sell tickets to his plays. Soon after that play was written, Elizabeth I's court ordered the theatres to be closed. It was nothing to do with him specifically, but because of the threat posed by the plague. It must have been obvious though that the monarch's officials could do that at any time and it had happened before. Shakespeare wrote to satisfy his patrons, firstly Elizabeth, the Virgin Queen, and then James I – both of them Tudor monarchs on whose largesse Shakespeare depended.

To: blooRuby@internet.com June 5th

Okay, I'll give you that one. Shakespeare elaborated for effect. Playwrights do that all the time. Richard was still a murderer though. He killed those two innocent little boys, the Princes in the Tower.

To: drunkellie@internet.com June 11th
Sorry it's been so long Ellie. I've been really busy but also I've been fuming at you tbh. Your last email just made me so cross. Sure Richard killed people in battle, he was reported to be a strong and valiant soldier, but the murder of his nephews, that's the biggest lie of all. When you went on to study science I thought you were taught to analyse things you read and verify for yourself, not just accept someone else's say so.

To: blooRuby@internet.com June 11th
Wow! I really struck a nerve didn't I? Tell you what, you explain to me how you're so sure that he didn't do it, and exactly who did. I'll listen, I might counter what you're saying but I'll definitely listen – can't say fairer than that, can I? We can't fall out over something that happened – how many years ago was it?

To: drunkellie@internet.com June 11th
Richard III was written in 1592. Do you know who was on the throne then? Elizabeth I, and she was a Tudor. Who fought against Richard and beat him at the Battle of Bosworth Field? Henry VII, the first Tudor monarch. The play was written over a hundred years after the reign of Richard III, in a time when very few people could read and write, information was largely passed on by word of mouth. Inaccuracies

must have been common.

To: blooRuby@internet.com June 13th

Hmm, Chinese Whispers. I did as I said and questioned everything you wrote so far, and you're quite right. Did you know that it wasn't just plague that threatened the theatres? The Puritans saw it as immoral and the players lived constantly under the threat of having their livelihoods removed.

That doesn't change things about the boys though does it? And I will keep coming back to this. Remember on the battlefield when he was losing he shouted *'A horse, a horse, my kingdom for a horse'*? He was a coward, desperate to get away. I bet he was terrified that the opposition, Henry Tudor wasn't it, would learn about those boys, and take his revenge. Henry was married to the boys' sister after all.

To: drunkellie@internet.com June 13th

I'm impressed, you've done your homework! Yes, Henry married young Elizabeth of York in 1486, but by that time Richard was already dead, and if he had killed the boys, then so must they be. To explain my reasoning about the boys I need to set the scene a little bit. Bear with me.

Richard never expected to be king. His oldest brother Edward IV was a tall, blond Adonis of a figure and he fancied the ladies, but he was only a lad of nineteen and very much under the thumb of his cousin, one of the power-hungry Nevill family. I told you about the power-hungry families, but I promise you Ellie, I'll try to only mention them when it's important to the story.

Edward IV was a lady's man, but he was very

keen on Elizabeth of York. Now she was part of the other powerful family I was talking about, the Woodvilles, and she was a very strong-willed lady. There was no way she would settle for anything less than marriage, and so he married her. Are you with me so far?

To: blooRuby@internet.com June 15th
Wow! It's complicated isn't it? I've got up a family tree on the internet, to help me get my head round them all. But none of this means that Richard couldn't have killed the boys, or I should say, had them killed. I looked it up and found that a man called Tyrrel confessed that he killed them on Richard's behalf, and he was put to death for it. Am I right? If so, I rest my case, Milady!

To: drunkellie@internet.com June 16th
At least I've got you thinking Ellie, that's good. And you're quite right about Tyrrel, *but* nobody who worked in the tower said that Tyrrel had been there, and surely they would know. How do you get two bodies, and these weren't babies remember, they were young teens, out of the tower without anyone knowing? It seems likely, and this is by no means definite, but there's nothing to show otherwise, that Tyrrel was set up – the fall guy. We know Richard himself can't have killed them because he was involved in a battle in the north at the time. (The last definite recording of them being alive was 1483) Do you know when Tyrrel was executed for his supposed part in the crime?

To: blooRuby@internet.com June 16th

Oh blast, Ruby. He wasn't put to death until 1502. That's nearly twenty years after the event. If they were so sure by the time Henry came to the throne, they'd have executed him straightaway surely? So what did happen to those boys?

To: drunkellie@internet.com June 16th

You're getting a bit ahead of the story. I've told you already Ellie, about the power-mad Nevilles. Now Richard III had married Anne Neville, the daughter of their cousin Richard Neville. Anne and Richard had largely been brought up together and were always very close, and together they had one son. Sadly though, as I've said, his wife and son died. This is important because the only way the Yorkist line could continue on the throne was by Richard's two nephews surviving him, growing up and having families of their own. So why on earth would he kill them?

To: blooRuby@internet.com June 17th

Okay, that's fine but surely Richard would be more bothered about saving himself than worrying about the Yorkist dynasty? And the other thing you haven't covered is, if not killed by Tyrrel at the request of Richard, then what happened to the boys? I know I keep coming back to that, but it was my original question a fortnight ago if you remember.

To: drunkellie@internet.com June 17th

I thought you'd pick up on the second point, and the answer has to be nobody knows for certain what happened to them, but there is a school of thought that by the time of the Battle of Bosworth

Field, in case things didn't go his way, Richard had already had the boys spirited away to the safety of a monastery in the north. Remember Richard had spent a lot of time in the north, he was known and trusted and had friends there.

As for trying to save himself, even your version courtesy of Shakespeare said that he shouted *'A horse, a horse, my kingdom for a horse'* at the Battle of Bosworth Field, so it seems likely that he had tried to save himself at that point.

To: blooRuby@internet.com June 17th
You're making a good case. But something happened to the boys, otherwise Edward IV would have been succeeded on the throne by his son Young Edward. Who killed them?

To: drunkellie@internet.com June 17th
That's the real question isn't it? But you're getting ahead of yourself again. Young Edward was twelve when his father died. He was too young to be crowned in his own right, but not by a lot. Edward IV had granted guardianship to Richard and there was even a coronation date set, so whoever had decided to remove the princes had to act quickly. Edward IV had also declared Richard as Protector of the Realm.

But then something else happened. Cue the soap opera music.

To: blooRuby@internet.com June 17th
I'd forgotten what a tease you are! Okay, soap opera episode over, the duff-duff music has played, let's get on to the next week's episode.

To: drunkellie@internet.com June 17th

The Bishop of Bath declared that he had something important to announce to parliament and a council was held on 8th June 1483, where he announced that Edward IV had been married already and had bigamously married Elizabeth Woodville. Therefore *all* his children, including the current heir, Young Edward, were illegitimate. What do you think of that? It is like a soap opera isn't it? Only these were real people, not made-up characters.

To: blooRuby@internet.com June 17th

So do tell, what difference does this make now? Are you sure about this by the way – could this bishop bloke have been telling porkies? What was in it for him?

To: drunkellie@internet.com June 17th

To answer the last questions first, no, there was no doubt. He had written evidence and he had nothing to gain from lying. He had performed the marriage ceremony between Edward and a Lady Eleanor Butler, and it was all logged there in the Parliamentary documents. As to what difference it made, it immediately made Edward IV's offspring illegitimate, and that disbarred them all from the throne. This meant that Neville's enemy Richard, whom Edward had made Protector of the Realm, would legitimately reign as king. As a result, Parliament declared Richard's entitlement to the throne in an Act called Titulus Regius and he was crowned a month later.

To: blooRuby@internet.com June 17th

Well I feel a bit deflated now. He was king, and there seems no reason for him to dispose of anybody.

To: drunkellie@internet.com   June 17th
Exactly my point, and furthermore Richard had dispatched emissaries to Rome, to have the boys' illegitimacy overturned. This would be so that if he should die, and it was fairly likely. The country was now in turmoil, and there was trouble brewing in France, (including from George, one of his older brothers) he wanted to secure a Yorkist on the throne, i.e. Young Edward. Not only was there no reason to kill the boys, there was evidence that he was trying to reinstate them.

To: blooRuby@internet.com June 17th
So, I accept it. I accept that he didn't kill the boys or have them killed. It still doesn't answer my original query. Who did, and why? In fact, were they killed at all, and if not, what happened?

To: drunkellie@internet.com June 18th
Nobody knows for sure, but there are some pointers. The whole of Parliament now knows about the illegitimacy. It's not just the boys, but their sister, young Elizabeth Woodville would be illegitimate too.
Now Henry Tudor, who was the one fomenting the uprisings in France and with Richard's older brother George, wanted to marry Young Elizabeth. Remember she was a born a Woodville and they were a very ambitious family – the women as much as the men. Now if Henry was to be king, which was his plan, he could not marry a bastard. If he did all his offspring would also be deemed as illegitimate

and debarred from the throne in the same way as the young princes had been. So he would have to legitimise her in order to marry her. He could not do that without also legitimising her brothers, and so automatically putting Young Edward on the throne. It was a Catch 22 for the future Henry VII and Elizabeth.

Young Edward's claim to the throne was much stronger than Henry's and he was in the way. I think Henry had the princes killed after Richard's death. He would have had the support of his future wife. How much better from her point of view to be the wife of a king, rather than just the sister of a king, with the younger brother waiting in the wings to inherit, should Young Henry die. And she was their sister. Nobody at the Tower would question her having access to them, taking them out etc.

To: blooRuby@internet.com June 18th
That certainly seems to make more sense than Richard doing it, but why do you say he had them killed *after Richard's death?*

To: drunkellie@internet.com June 18th
From Bosworth Field, as soon as Richard was dead, Henry VII came straight to the Tower of London. (Remember that was a royal palace, not merely a prison) There's no evidence of any reports of the boys being dead or missing at that stage. All that comes out much later. In the meantime Henry is crowned king and the House of Tudor is firmly established on the throne. Henry's entitlement was pretty slim. He wasn't of royal blood, only inheriting through marriage. (Edward IV and Richard III, and

therefore the young princes, could trace their lineage back to Edward III via five different lines.)

If the boys were already dead or missing it would have greatly enhanced Henry's justification for having killed the popular Richard, if he had brought it to the public's notice by immediately accusing Richard, and yet he said nothing.

And so we come to friend Shakespeare, who was paid not to put forward his own ideas, but to toe the party line, in this case the Tudor party line. To have written the truth, that the Tudors were ruling without entitlement would be foolish and probably would have condemned him to death. Shakespeare had a household and family in Stratford to support, a household in London and a troupe of actors depending on him for their livelihood remember.

Did you ever watch that TV programme *Who do you think you are?* where famous people trace their ancestry? Who would be foolish enough to suggest to our current monarch that Danny Dyer or Alexander Armstrong may have the stronger claim to the current throne because they can trace their roots directly back to Edward III?

There will be those who gainsay the ideas put forward, but there is a strong level of support amongst historians for Richard III's innocence.

To: blooRuby@internet.com June 18th
Including me, Ruby. Including me.

Doggone It!

Our favourite morning walk, well mine and I suppose Anna's too, is along the disused railway track. Anna is always secured safely at the end of the dog lead of course, so there is no danger of wandering off, chasing rabbits or squirrels, which is a favourite hobby.

Since this crazy pandemic hit, that has had people wearing masks and stinking of hand-sanitiser, there has been a lot of talk about dogs. People who suddenly were forced to spend time at home instead of in stuffy offices must have thought: *This is a great time to get a dog, then when this is over, I can go back to the office and the dog can go ...?* just where exactly? That seems to be the bit that some of them haven't thought through yet.

As we walked down to the track we'd meet all these news dogs we'd never seen before, lots of them barely old enough to be out and about in my opinion, but we would just greet them from a safe distance and then carry on our usual explorations.

The railway track was a good place to walk with Anna. Trains can't turn round sharp corners, so any bends are very gentle, which means that people – and it's people that are spreading these viruses, not dogs – can be seen coming from a distance away, and avoided. Anna has got very good at it now. A short tug on the lead from me and she steps off the tracks and into the shrubbery at the side whenever there's someone approaching. The other advantage of this walk is that trains don't readily climb steep hills and so it's fairly flat. So although we can walk miles and miles, it's not too difficult, and let's face it, neither Anna nor I are getting any younger.

One night last week we had both eaten and were curled up together in the chair watching television when an alarming item came on the news. It was pointing out my concerns about what was going to happen to all these newly-acquired dogs post-lockdown, but it also went on to talk about how dogs were being stolen. It seemed like lots and lots of dogs were being stolen. Sometimes they were being stolen to order, specific breeds, and the item explained how these thieves were approaching dog walkers, particularly women walking alone, snatching the dog and having a car parked nearby to make their getaway.

It seemed to me that the item was like a *How To* guide, just giving people ideas on how to steal dogs. Judging from Anna's face she thought the same. Not that she said anything of course, but I hope she felt the same as me, that we belonged together.

I thought about our walks along the track. I hoped we wouldn't have to change our usual routine and walk around the town for safety. Safer for dogs maybe but not so much for their humans. It gets so busy with people and not all of them keep their distance like they're supposed to. The footpaths are harder underfoot too, and it's quite hilly. There aren't the lovely country smells and views either. No, I wanted to stick to the railway line.

This morning we set off as usual, after the usual checks of course: Poo bags, mask, keys, handkerchief, phone, disinfectant wipes – yes, we had everything we needed.

The railway line has two crossings on the route we take. Not proper level crossings with gates and things like the one in the village, but what I had once heard called *Occupational Crossings.* They seemed to be where paths, I suppose used by farmers who owned the land, crossed so they could reach their fields on the other side. A little further along from these a bridge passed over this disused line. Sometimes we went up on that bridge to have a change, and through the nearby farmyard. You had to watch out for cars and tractors up there though, something that wasn't a problem on the tracks. There was a lovely collie living at the farm. She was so well behaved and obedient. She put my efforts at training to shame.

It was just on the far side of this bridge that disaster struck this morning. Anna and I had kept a close eye out for people approaching and twice we had stepped out of the way into the bushes. The second time an approaching dog walker had done the same, so for a moment or two we were both hiding in the shrubbery about twenty metres apart, which was funny and also a bit ridiculous. But then we emerged from under the bridge with the lead extended to its full three metres to allow for undergrowth snuffling. A young man appeared, seemingly from nowhere but actually from behind the bridge archway. He must have climbed down from the top of the bridge. A quick look round showed that the other dog walkers were now out of sight and probably out of hearing range, but someone had come up behind us, another youth who presumably had slid down from the other side of the bridge's parapet.

I was very cross. These two lowlifes had made Anna afraid and I could see her trembling. Before I could do anything to save her, the first youth had taken out a pair of scissors and snipped through the dog lead, right next to the collar. The remaining lead retracted uselessly, and the youth looped two fingers through the dog collar and retained a firm hold.

I was amazed at what happened next. Anna turned and elbowed the second boy in the stomach, hard. She is only a little woman and her elbows were just the right height. With an *Ooof!* noise he dropped to his knees in the mud and doubled over. I looked at his companion and could see his Adam's Apple bobbing up and down. He didn't know what to do. He dropped the scissors and I put my foot on them and growled at him.

There was a clicking sound and I pricked up my ears and turned towards it. Anna had taken her phone out of her pocket and taken photographs of them both, and then pressed some of the buttons. She'd taken photos of me before, so I'm sure that's what she did.

Then she shouted at the phone: 'I'm being attacked by two kids trying to steal my dog.' She went on to tell the phone exactly where we were, but surely the phone knew that, it was here with us. Then she closed the phone-case, shouted, 'Catch,' and I leapt up and caught it in my teeth, growling deeply when the first youth attempted to take it off me.

But Anna was not finished yet. She had something else in her pocket, and it stank. I wanted to sneeze, but she hadn't given me the command, *Drop it*, so I had to keep holding onto the phone.

She took the stinky stuff and squirted it, first on the figure kneeling on the ground, on his hair and on his jacket. The other one was reaching for the scissors, trying to push me off them, but I stayed put and Anna came and squirted him too, all over his hair and then, as he turned to run away, on his shoes and the bottom of his jeans.

At home, as we sat, Anna nursing a hot drink, and me having wolfed down a pile of dog treats, the police person said we had done very well as Anna explained to them what had happened. She had shown them the photographs when they first arrived on the railway track. The second boy hadn't moved once Anna told me to stand guard over him, until the police had carted him away. I'm a big softy really but I can have scary teeth when I want to, even when I'm holding a phone.

Sleepily I half listened to the conversation. Anna told the police that years ago she had taken some self-defence lessons and had been able to hit one of them. The other one had run away and gone home, but the police already had a good idea who they were looking for, and when they said a name to his mate, it was confirmed. When they got there he still stank of Anna's perfume, the stinky stuff she only uses if she's getting poshed up to go out. I hate that smell, it means she's leaving me for a few hours, but it had come in handy this morning.

In the back garden of the smelly youth's house they found some dogs and young puppies shut in sheds, and they also said they found lists of names and telephone numbers with dog breeds written down next to them. They talked to the neighbours who said that there always seemed to be dogs coming and going, this had been going on since the beginning of lockdown.

The man had been really cheeky to the police, said the smelly perfume was what he called *an offensive weapon* and that he wanted them to prosecute Anna for carrying it.

'Oh really,' Anna laughed when the officers told her, 'It's not an offensive weapon, I looked on the internet and know it's an offence to carry a weapon. This is just the dregs of an old bottle of perfume I took to show my friend yesterday evening. I'd forgotten to take it out of my coat pocket, that's all. Have another ginger biscuit?'

And she had winked at them, and threw a ginger biscuit to me on the rug.

Just for the Record

Joseph had always been a somewhat precocious child, walking and talking early. She had read all the books she could find on child development and how to encourage individuality.

In line with the current philosophy on child rearing she tried to let him know in advance when she had anything planned, especially if it interfered with what he wanted to do. He was very single minded and determined and occasionally she even managed to fend off a tantrum.

And so, as she placed a plate of fish fingers and mashed potatoes in front of Joseph, she said: 'Just for the record, after lunch we will be going into town on the bus. I have some shopping to do.'

She found herself watching anxiously for his response, but he merely nodded and addressed himself to the fish fingers.

Taking it for a win, she washed their lunch pots, washed his hands and combed his hair then went out to the bus stop.

Joseph loved the bus ride. She had a car but it was a treat for him to go by bus and the front upstairs seat was available, which was a bonus.

The problems started when they got back home. Joseph's tantrum started almost immediately, and he was inconsolable.

It was several minutes before the sobbing and sniffling became quiet enough to be able to hear him, but even now his mother had no idea what he was talking about.

'We didn't get it,' he hiccoughed, 'we never got it and we went to town specially.'

'Never got what, Joseph?' His mother thought back over their purchases. She had ticked off everything on her shopping list. Whatever was the child talking about? She hadn't the least idea.

At last the sobbing reduced to a muffled sniffling, 'The birthday present for Grandad,' he said at last, as if this was some sort of explanation and it was obvious, but his mother was still in the dark.

'What birthday present, Joseph? It's weeks yet till Grandad's birthday. I haven't even thought about what to get him. What made you think we were getting it today?'

'You said, you promised. You know how Grandad loves music and you said,' he gulped, 'You said that we were getting him some music this afternoon.'

His mother shook her head, but the tears were threatening again.

'Okay love. I think one of us must have got mixed up.'

Joseph turned belligerent, 'Mummy, you said

we were going to town to get some music for Grandad's birthday.'

'I don't think I did. What did I say exactly? Can you remember?'

'Yes,' he snuffled, 'I was sitting at the table eating and you said: *Just for the record, we're going into town on the bus after lunch.* You said it, Mummy, We were going to town just to get a record for Grandad.'

Victoriana

The bathtub groaned and shifted slightly on its ancient claw feet. Never before had the one they all called "Mummy" turned its taps on so viciously, so hard, and then left the room.

Water was gushing so quickly into its cavernous body that the bathtub had hardly heard that insistent, intermittent chirruping of the phone, that the mummy always seemed unable to ignore. But she had heard it, sworn under her breath, and hurried from the room, leaving the water to get on with it.

The pipes and taps attached to the bathtub were much newer than the tub itself, and this was what was so worrying.

For more – much more – than a century the bathtub had done its job well. It had coped with the hygiene firstly of a Victorian family. Then the bathtub was brand new, the first fixed tub that family had known, and it was treated reverentially, with the children exhorted not to scratch it and not to turn on the taps themselves while the big people weren't in the room, or they would either burn or drown.

The bathtub wanted to object. Touching the taps would not hurt the children, and if they put their hands in the hot water they would be scalded not burned. But of course bathtubs cannot talk, and therein lay the problem now.

As it reflected on the past, the pipes beneath shifted slightly under the increasing weight of the water and one emitted a painful groan.

The bathtub sighed. The next family whom it had owned had been less considerate. There had, it seemed, been dozens of little humans, although common sense suggested only four. They seemed to use the bathtub in relays, two by two and there were constant battles about whose turn it was to sit at the window end, and whose toy boat or duck was the broken one. These encounters had happened only once a week which was just as well, as it took the bathtub that long to recover from the onslaught of kicks and thumps, and from the noise-induced headache.

Now the smart modern taps, new but meant to look old like the original ones, gave a spluttery cough, as if they too realised that there was something wrong – they had been working for far too long on this one fill.

The hot tap was beginning to feel its intestines run cooler and cooler, as if the central heating boiler too had exhausted its potential. The bathtub shifted imperceptibly. One of its claw feet had been damaged slightly when it was removed from its first home, and although none of the humans had even noticed this, that ankle occasionally hurt; when the cleaner rubbed at it too hard for instance, or perhaps when the bathroom was exceptionally cold, cold enough to make the metal feet contract. This bathroom was lovely and warm, the constantly-heated towel rail made sure that the bathtub was always comfortable.

It wasn't comfortable now. The damaged claw foot ached under the weight and the bathtub felt ready to explode, it was so full. And then what would happen? The house would flood; maybe the floor would collapse, the bathtub felt so bloated and heavy.

The taps, unable to stop, were still gushing – cold water issuing from both now that the hot tank was empty. The water level was lapping noisily round the little overflow outlet but anyone could see that the water was rushing into the tub much faster than it was escaping through this tiny hatch. The water snatched at a facecloth draped over the tub's roll-top, and this danced and gyrated under the taps, changing the timbre of the beating water, but not alleviating the threat.

Just as the bathtub was sure that this was the end, that it would explode under the pressure and land in pieces in the destroyed kitchen below and from there be consigned to a skip, its human Mummy came back into the room.

'Oh, no!' She snatched the plug with one hand and quickly turned off the taps with the other. The water swirled and swore angrily as it was swallowed by the plughole, and the bathtub felt an immediate relief of pressure and worry.

Disaster had been averted – this time.

Twins

Okay I'm not afraid to say it, I hate being one of twins. I've always hated it from as young an age as I can remember. To put you in the picture, I am one of a pair of what is called fraternal twins. That means that we don't necessarily look alike, sound alike, think alike or share anything more than any other brothers and sisters do. We could even be of different genders – one a boy and one a girl, but we're not. To be honest life might be easier for me if we were. People, strangers often, would comment, *It must be lovely always to have someone you're so in tune with,* or *You must miss Estella when she's not around, feel like you've a limb missing!* What would they say I wonder if I'd honestly said, *'Yes, I miss her like you miss a headache when it finally goes, dreading that it may return.'* How ungrateful that would sound, how bitchy.

I do sound really bitchy don't I? I don't mean to, it just seems that some people are more fortunate than others, and when it's your twin that's the fortunate one, I guess it has an effect on you and the relationship between you. And yes, my twin is really called Estella. Smart name, huh? Classy. Her name exhausted our parents' ingenuity in terms of their decision making powers, and they called me – their second-born by twenty minutes – Jane. Not very imaginative is it?

It might not have been so bad had I been born first. That's something of an achievement isn't it? To have thrust your way assertively into the world, the foremost, the strongest, leaving Estella to tag along behind. But no, I simply glided into existence, riding as it were on her coat tails, she smoothing the way for me. That's the first and last time that happened I can tell you.

Jane suits me, just plain Jane. Childhood photographs bear out the startling contrast. It isn't all just my toxic poisoned brain misremembering. Images show Estella, petite and pretty, with tumbling blonde curls and blue eyes. My face isn't hideous or grotesque, just androgynous and forgettable.

Perhaps if I'd been born a boy the comparisons would have been less odious. I take after our father, in fact I could be his double give or take thirty years. I'm big, I'm clumsy, I'm heavy and my hair is a nondescript wispy mud-colour.

I remember a rhyme someone said or perhaps I read it somewhere, I forget now. I never forgot the rhyme though. It goes:

I have a sister Jennifer and she is very pretty
Where I am Jane and very plain, now isn't that
a pity?

Photographs of us growing up demonstrated my mother's continuing lack of imagination. I don't know whether identical twins like to be displayed in identical outfits, but I know I didn't, and yet it was my mother's go-to for every event and activity throughout our childhood until I was old enough to rebel, and all were obviously chosen to suit Estella. She even kept one pair of dresses, beautiful dresses that we had worn for somebody's wedding. I took them out of their box on one occasion when I was about nine. One bore a label saying Age 3-4; the other one Age 5-6. No prizes for guessing who wore which.

My mum and dad never seemed to rate my achievements, and blow me, wasn't Estella just as clever. You may think I'm exaggerating or that this is sour grapes, but I remember one occasion when I must have been about seven or eight. I had learned to spell Estella, and very pleased with myself, went to tell my mum. E-S-T-E-L-L-A. I was especially pleased to have remembered the double-L.

Now, my middle name is Lynda, with a Y. My mum's response to my pride? 'And can you spell Lynda?'

I'd never thought about it but, buoyed up by my success, I gave it a go, L-I-N-D-E-R. My mother just looked at me and said, 'learning your own name would be a lot more impressive than learning your sister's.'

Estella had been promised a new bike if she passed the exam that got her a place in grammar school.

My dad had gone so far as to put my name down

for the local private secondary school as he didn't think I was going to pass the eleven plus exam. He stressed on me what a good school it was and how it would be important for me to work hard so I could get a good job. I had a bit of a laugh, but only to myself, when it wasn't me but Estella who failed the exam and I went off to the grammar school – not clever, but intelligent enough to get by.

Of course he had to stand by his promise to her, and buy me a new bike. Needless to say Estella got a new bike as well and the gilt was taken off that gingerbread a little when I overheard my mum on the phone to her oldest friend.

'Thank goodness,' I heard her say from my listening post at the turn of the stairs, 'We're not worried about Estella of course, she's so pretty she's bound to marry young and won't have to keep herself for long.' So that was it. The assumption that because she was dainty and petite and pretty she would marry her prince at an early age and live happily ever after, whilst I would have to earn my own crusts, an embittered old spinster. Not that it was something that worried me at eleven years old.

There is something else that stands out from about that time though. Estella and I were fortunate enough to each have our own bedroom, and it seemed that I was already developing into someone who didn't need a lot of sleep. I had asked for bookshelves from my parents for my birthday, and relatives had been delighted to give me book tokens as presents – the easy way out. Often I would read myself to sleep, but one evening I had done something to upset Estella and she turned bitchy. She shouted downstairs to our mum and dad, 'Jane's still got her light on.' I looked at the clock, it was nearly midnight. Up stomped my dad. Seriously I don't think he wanted to get cross, and he pulled the covers back looking for the book, although he didn't find it as I had hidden it under my pillow. He read the Riot Act and told me that I would have no pocket money for three weeks.

Next day I was still annoyed about it, it seemed so unfair to be told off for something so obviously harmless and nobody can fall asleep to order. Estella had evidently been awake too, my little bedside lamp wasn't bright enough to have disturbed her on the other side of the house, but no-one had thought to comment on that had they? I waited till we were sitting at the breakfast table then I said, 'When I grow up I'm only going to have one child,' I looked at their faces around the table, I had their attention, 'and I hope she's the type of child who reads quietly, disturbing nobody if she can't get to sleep at night, rather than the kind who snitches and runs to Mummy and Daddy to tell tales.'

You could have heard a pin drop. Nobody knew what to say. I think because it made a lot of sense. It did to me anyway. Then Estella burst into tears and ran to her bedroom with Mum in pursuit. Dad just sighed wearily then he and I finished our meal in silence. Needless to say it was considerably more than three weeks before my pocket money was reinstated.

*　　*　　*

I've already told you that I was, even as a child, one of those people who don't seem to need a great deal of sleep, so when I put my bike to good use and got a paper round at the age of thirteen, it was no problem to me getting up early. And it had to be early. My dad insisted that I have at least a hot drink before I went out, and the newsagent I worked for had his shop on the far side of town.

I loved being out so early whatever the weather. It was as if the whole world belonged to me. Not that it was easy. My round included some of the biggest properties in the area, mostly with huge gardens and even a tennis court or two. On Sundays particularly, with all the supplements, I could barely push the bike with its load, never mind ride it, and sometimes I had to make two trips.

If I say so myself I was very reliable, and fairly frugal. Each week I saved at least half my wages. I'm not sure what I was saving for but it just seemed sensible, and it was reassuring to see the balance in my post office account gradually growing. Of course Estella never had any money left over by the end of the week. Make-up, tights and going out with friends were expensive and she would often beg to borrow five pounds or whatever. My parents would tell me I was mean if I had the money and wouldn't help out my sister who hadn't, but borrowing rarely meant repaying in Estella's world and you can see why I said I hated being a twin.

It wasn't all bad though. Estella was popular and as her twin I was generally including in her exciting world; at the periphery of it anyway, and felt less lonely than I perhaps otherwise would have. This was my chance to ride on her coat tails in a good way.

But then inevitably boys came into the equation. Pretty Estella, confident and used to socialising and making   friends,   moved   seamlessly   through adolescence and then began dating Thomas.

My social crutch had deserted me. Estella and Thomas were out together most evenings and the crowd of friends who had always surrounded her forgot to call round when there was only me to come and talk to.

* * *

My enjoyment of the paper round ended abruptly one December morning just two weeks before our sixteenth birthday. It all started quite normally, then I reached one of the larger houses called The Corner, because it was, fairly obviously, located on a corner in the road. It was very lonely, half way up a cul-de sac, with large banks of rhododendron bushes edging the drive. As I got to the middle of this dense shrubbery a man suddenly appeared from the garage door. I had seen him before over the years but today he was wearing a dressing gown over pyjamas.

I'm not going to relive here that horrible experience at the hands of a man old enough to be my grandfather. Suffice it to say he touched me inappropriately, kissed me – ugh! and told me very graphically what he would like to do to me. I was so shocked that I shouted the first thing to come into my head, 'But I'm only fifteen.' He winked at me, licked his lips and said, 'Soon then,' as I jumped on my bike and rode off.

As soon as I got home I told my dad what had happened, and to his credit he immediately phoned the shop. I listened on the stairs to his half of the conversation and it was obvious that Mr Halford the newsagent was sceptical. My father said things like, *I know, she's very immature,* and *Of course he's a highly respected businessman.* I think that was the first time I realised that in life I would have to look out for myself.

The next day I went into the shop as usual.

'Feeling better?'

'No, Mr Halford, not really, I'm feeling very let down actually.' I wasn't sure how these things should be done but I handed him a note I had written out. 'That's my notice. The last day I work will be two weeks today, and I will only work the two weeks if you take out the papers for The Corner and have someone else deliver them.' I was pleased that I sounded a lot more confident than I felt.

Absently he extracted the relevant newspaper from the pile, then asked, 'what if I can't find anyone else to deliver it?'

'Then you'll have to find someone else to deliver the whole round, as from today.'

He put the paper to one side and picked up the note, 'You can't do this, Jane. This means your last day would be Saturday twenty-third of December. That's just before Christmas.'

'I know.'

The next two weeks of interaction between us was carried out in silence, and the newspapers to be delivered to The Corner were not in my bag. On the twenty-third I went into the shop and waited for my wages.

Mr Halford handed them over and watched me count what was in the envelope. He had a second envelope in his hand.

'These are your Christmas tips that have been brought into the shop, I'm not sure you deserve them. If you want to know what I think, I'd say you have a lot of growing up to do young lady.'

I put my hand out for the envelope, 'I think tips are usually paid for a good service that has already been given, not as a bribe to deliver a good service in the future so I have definitely earned those tips. For three years I have trekked through all weathers to make sure people got their newspapers every morning. I have done a double round when other people have not come in, or have been ill. I've struggled on Sundays when the papers were so heavy I had to make two trips, and I've never complained. I've earned those tips.' He handed the envelope over, but I wasn't done yet, 'As for growing up, I've grown up a lot in the last two weeks. I've learned that you can't rely on grown-ups to fight your corner – you have to do that for yourself.'

*   *   *

That night I set my alarm clock for two hours later than normal, although I couldn't stay in bed that long. When I got down to the kitchen my dad was eating breakfast,

'Jane, whatever's the matter. Why aren't you out on your paper round?'

'I've finished my paper round. Mr Halford let me down and I don't choose to work for him anymore.' I didn't say *And so did you,* but it hung in the air anyway. That morning I went into town to a small jewellery shop and secured a Saturday job for myself.

What else was there for me to do but read school textbooks and do the set homework and revision? So by the time I left school I had at least some A levels to my name. Estella had left school after GCSEs and worked answering the phone in a local office. She and Thomas were saving up.

When I first asked about university Dad wasn't sure. I found that I was looking down on him as we faced off in the kitchen, as I was now an inch taller than him. 'Look at me Dad, there's no Thomas lurking in the wings waiting to steal my heart, I'm going to have to fend for myself.' He didn't argue.

I remember my first year at uni was just coming to an end. It had been enjoyable and hard work in equal measure. I was sitting writing a letter trying to secure an internship with a city architect firm for my second year, when I was called to the Junior Common Room phone.

It was Estella. She'd never bothered to ring before. Occasionally she just scrawled a couple of lines at the bottom of Mum's weekly letters, usually just moaning that she and Thomas hardly ever went out because of all the money they needed to save, they never had any fun. My thoughts immediately went to Mum and Dad. Something must have happened to one of them.

'Erm, there's nothing wrong Jane, nothing to worry about.' At least she said that first, 'I just wanted to let you know that Thomas and I will be getting married sooner than we originally planned.' There was a pause, 'In three weeks' time actually.'

Selfish Jane, I spoke my first thought out loud,

'But I'll be just starting exams, I have revision sessions. I can't possibly come home in three weeks. Why three weeks anyway?' and then the penny dropped, 'Oh, you're pregnant! You silly goose!'

'Thomas and I are delighted about the news obviously,' her voice sounded strained, 'and I can't do anything about the three weeks, we have to get married before his Mum and Dad find out about the baby. We need their permission because we're not twenty-one yet and Thomas's dad has always threatened to cut him off if he let the family down.

'Anyway, it's not as if you were going to be a bridesmaid or anything, my two friends from school are doing that, so you're not missing out on anything special.'

I stayed quiet. Of course I hadn't expected to be a bridesmaid, the photographs would have looked ridiculous, I stood nearly a foot taller than Estella and her two friends, and at least six inches taller than Thomas, but it had never occurred to me that I wouldn't be at their wedding as a guest.

'Couldn't you miss a day's college and come down for the ceremony?' she sounded distinctly unenthusiastic.

'What? Travel all that way after lectures on the Friday night, spend the day at a boozy celebration then catch the snail train back on Sunday before a week of full-on exams? I don't think so. I'll send you · a card.'

My little nephew is a delight, although I don't see much of him. It's as if Estella knows I've seen through her surface persona to the vapid character underneath. She has thoroughly compartmentalised her life and keeps me away from her domestic bliss.

At least I hope it is bliss for her. It would be awful to go through a marriage and motherhood to be miserable, although I doubt she's as happy as I am.

I have my own friends now in the city, and am in talks about going into partnership next year with Theo, a student I met in my second year. We have plans to take the London architectural scene by storm.

Theo is intelligent and kind, and ugly in an attractive sort of way. He is also very tall and for the first time in my life I feel quite feminine and protected. He values my brain and my input into our shared projects. Who knows whether one day we may marry, neither of us are in a hurry.

There's more to life than rushing into these things, and there's certainly more to life than outward appearances.

And if I should have a family, especially if I should have twins, I will make sure that I never dress them alike, and I shall value each of them for what sets them apart.

Two little Ducks

George and Charlie had a relationship based on trust, and an unwritten agreement. One of those that evolves organically between two people in tune with each other. They never checked each other's laptop. Nor did they open each other's post or emails. Even when George was working away he would come home to a neat pile of letters on the hall table with the date received scribbled on the corner of each envelope, as if Charlie were his secretary, not his partner. If anything had looked important Charlie would ask on one of their frequent phone calls, and only open it if he told her to go ahead. He would proudly tell anyone who asked that it was all about trust, an intrinsic foundation of their relationship.

This time was necessarily different. George had dropped Charlie off at the hospital for what he was assured was a routine operation, with an anticipated stay of five days. The pandemic meant that there would be no visiting, so George now had time on his hands until she called to be collected.

He arrived home from the hospital to a couple of letters on the mat. This was quite rare these days, and getting more so as electronic communication took over modern lives.

He threw the rubbish in the bin, but one letter addressed to Charlie was evidently important, and he was undecided about what to do. It was obviously something official, with a return address stamped on the flap, for if it was not delivered. The front of the letter had a red banner in the corner that read:

Urgent. Not a circular. Open immediately

Now George was in a quandary. He thought about phoning Charlie and asking her permission to read the letter to her, but she may already have moved into that microcosm which is hospital life, that insulated bubble, which makes the rest of the world temporarily unimportant. He left the letter to one side, she would be home in five days, surely it would wait that long. Yet as he prepared for bed, making a hot drink, taking the dog for a last walk, then checking that the doors and windows were locked, the letter seemed to taunt him.

In particular that red banner seemed to have grown bigger and more threatening. He toyed again with the idea of phoning Charlie, but hospital hours were a law unto themselves, and she may well have settled for the night. He would leave it for now.

In the morning the nagging doubt was still there. He tried her phone after breakfast but it went straight to voicemail. He glanced at his watch. What happened before an operation? She would no doubt have another Covid test; no breakfast of course but a visit from the anaesthetist prior to the pre-med. Some time today she would be going to the theatre, but it could be any minute now or at five o'clock in the afternoon.

He tried several times to speak to Charlie during the day. Once the phone was engaged, but every other time there was no reply. Maybe her battery was flat, she had taken the charger but he had no idea what facilities were available to patients. If she was bed-bound could she even reach a plug socket?

Charlie seemed very remote. This must be what it was like for her when he used to work away for long periods. Then he gave himself a mental shake. She was only in hospital for five days for goodness sake. He laughed aloud at his silliness, making the dog jump.

On their afternoon walk to the recreation ground, he suddenly realised that the fifth day would be Friday. If Charlie couldn't be collected until later in the day – he had been told he would be given a specific time to collect her – then logically it could be Monday before the business responsible for the letter was available to contact. That would be a full week since it hit the doormat, not George's idea of immediate at all.

At last on the Tuesday evening he could bear it no longer. He was no doubt getting worked up about nothing, he had a tendency to do that according to Charlie. It was probably just a circular with an attention-grabbing headline. Having once more tried the telephone, he ripped that envelope open without ceremony and that's when his world fell apart.

At first the print would not keep still for him to read it, but he made out some of the words:

Exceed, overdraft limit, foreclose; bailiff

George dropped into the nearest chair and forced himself to read the letter slowly. He and Charlie had always kept their money separate. It had seemed logical when they first got together, and when he worked away so much for years. George now realised that he didn't even know how much Charlie earned. He picked up the envelope in a daze. There was no outward indication that it was from the bank, just this red message of doom and urgency on the front. He checked the name and address, just in case … but of course it was correct, it had not been wrongly delivered. The letter was definitely for his partner and he had no idea why.

There was little sleep that night. He spent some time looking for Charlie's bank statements, perhaps they would flag up the error that had undoubtedly occurred. The folder labelled *Bank* in her drawer of the filing cabinet was empty, and he had a vague recollection of times when her bank statement had arrived, been given a fairly cursory glance, then shredded almost at once. He had seen nothing unusual in this. Charlie was the type of person who disliked clutter, and would not hang on to things *Just in Case*, unlike George who kept lots of bits and pieces and documents all over the house. He tended to shred his bank statements only when the folder became so bulky it threatened to collapse.

At three o'clock in the morning he stretched out on the sofa, more to reassure a now anxious dog than

111

anything. He thought back over their thirty years together. The dog jumped up beside him and snuggled down.

He and Charlie had met when each had accompanied their parents to a Beetle Drive at the local chapel hall. He remembered his father being against the event, deeming it irreverent to gamble on chapel premises, but he had been overruled by those who felt the need to raise funds was more important. They had both loved the event, bartering for matchsticks and had since often visited the local coastal resort to go to the pier and play the slot machines. They had joked when people asked how they met, telling them they met through gambling at an event his father thought was the work of the devil. Eyebrows would be raised in surprise until they explained the reality.

Now George resolved on a plan of action. He would try to get some sleep, then in the morning he would contact the bank, explain the situation and see what they could tell him.

*   *   *

It was entirely by coincidence, although it seemed to George to be some malevolent fate that the following morning Charlie's credit card bill arrived. This time there was no hesitation. Three attempts at calling Charlie had proved fruitless and it was too early to phone the bank. This time there could be no mistake, the figures were very clear. Charlie had almost reached the maximum borrowing on her card, and the company was requesting a fifty per cent payment immediately as the balance was insufficient

112

to cover the next month's interest. He sat for a moment looking at the covering letter and read the horrific details, *Interest of twenty-four per cent.* How could they possibly justify that? Of course, they didn't have to, Charlie must have signed up to their agreement and those were the terms she had accepted.

He phoned the bank, but got no further, No, they were unable to discuss their client's affairs with him without her express permission, which they had not received. Was he her husband? No, her partner, then they could tell him nothing. Did he have Power of Attorney? No, then they could tell him nothing. Could they speak to Charlie, they had been asking her to get in touch for some time.

George didn't dare ask what they meant by *some time.* He explained the situation, said she was due out of hospital at the weekend and would be in contact on Monday to sort it out, would they please make a note of that? They would.

He breathed a sigh of relief. At least he would not have to panic about bailiffs for the next three days. It seemed like the first proper breath he had taken since the previous morning. He checked his phone, no message from Charlie, but one from the ward clerk. She was out of theatre. The operation had been successful and she was now sleeping peacefully.

George had hardly thought about Charlie as a person for over twenty-four hours. She had been transformed into this elephant in the room, this mountain of debt that somehow had to be dealt with. And Charlie had no idea that George knew about it. He felt as guilty as if he had been searching for something to hold against her, when that wasn't the case at all.

The week dragged, not just because Charlie wasn't around and the dog was clearly pining, but because of this great black cloud. He phoned her a couple of times, and was going to mention the letters, but she sounded so fragile and tearful that he decided nothing was to be gained from upsetting her further. Let her get home and they would tackle the problem together.

*   *   *

Charlie sat with her feet up on the sofa, the dog curled on her knee. George had silently handed her the two open letters then gone into the kitchen while she read them. He came back with two mugs of tea, and saw the tears in her eyes.

'You're a saint George, she said, 'Most men would have changed the locks and told me to get lost. I'm so sorry. I just seemed to get deeper and deeper in debt. With the rate of interest it just spirals, and you think you can deal with it, you think you can put it right.'

'I've looked in your wardrobe, Charlie. You've not bought anything new in a while. Your car's nine years old, we haven't been on holiday for over a year. You don't drink or smoke or take drugs. Where on earth has the money gone?'

Reluctantly she handed over her phone, and he counted three, four, no five gambling sites, all regularly visited and paid for on-line. No wonder he hadn't been aware of what was going on. He thought back to all the evenings they sat in their respective chairs, noses in their phones. He would be looking at the News headlines, Facebook, Twitter; checking emails and sometimes playing a game of Solitaire. And all the time Charlie had been gambling, wall to wall gambling. Probably sometimes winning and putting her winnings back into the process for another go-round.

'I kept thinking I just needed one big win, and then I could pay it all off and never gamble again,' she whispered, 'It doesn't work like that though, the win is never nearly enough and you tell yourself you're on a lucky streak to have won anything at all, if you plough it back in, maybe the next win will be the one that frees you from all the debt and all the worry.' She put her hands over her face.

He opened his mouth to tell her it was a mug's game, that the casino always wins, but then he closed it again. Charlie wasn't stupid, she knew all that. She also knew that gambling was an addiction, one that was hard to break.

Since a change in the law in 2007 there has been almost hourly advertising on television for all forms of gambling – on horse racing, football match scores, and Charlie's weapon of choice, bingo. The issues had quickly become apparent of course, and companies rushed to advertise so-called advice on not getting into debt, taking time out from gambling, setting financial limits and so on, but when one was addicted there was little motivation to introduce these strictures.

Charlie was tired but wanted to talk it out. They agreed to visit the bank together, where she thought the debt ran into thousands. George would be able to transfer some money to start paying that off and they could come up with a plan to deal with the rest eventually. Together they would draft a letter to the credit card company, and there and then Charlie cut the card into pieces.

She also gave George control of her phone. They set a very low limit of money she could gamble each week, and he set a password on the single remaining casino app she retained, so she had to ask him to unlock it before she started gambling.

Charlie found a local group of Gamblers' Anonymous, and in the same building on the same evening was a meeting of Gam-Anon, supporting friends and family of gamblers.

So they would spend one evening a week in their separate meetings, but agreed that they would not necessarily discuss what conversations had taken place there. At the end of the meetings they would collect a take-away meal and hopefully agree that the evening had been a success.

They were both aware that there was nothing to stop her, once she was again solvent, from buying another phone and starting up the many apps again. There was nothing to stop her calling at the betting shop on the way home from work, nor from going into one of the two casinos in town whenever she went shopping.

But George had faith in her. After all, theirs was a relationship based on trust.

Perchance to Dream

Vivien came out of the dentist's surgery feeling more despondent than ever. The new crown was going to cost more than she had in her bank account by over £300, and she'd be lucky if the car passed its MOT next month without having to spend money on it.

With a resigned sigh she set off down the alleyway to the car park. It was nearly time to pick up Lisa from nursery. Half way down the path she noticed something on the floor in front of her, and stooped to pick it up. It was a bulging unsealed envelope. As she looked at it, a woman entered the path from the opposite end and stopped to watch what Vivien was doing. Vivien opened the flap and saw a wad of notes, money, currency, mullah. Her heart leapt.

'Wow! That's a lot of dosh,' said the woman who had now reached the same place.

Vivien looked around, 'Is there a police station in the village? It closed down didn't it, a few years ago.'

That's right,' the woman said, not taking her eyes from the money. 'What are you going to do with it?'

Vivien glanced at her watch, 'First I have to collect my daughter from nursery, then I'll have to go into town to the police station there.'

'I could take it into the shop for you if you like, save you the trouble if you're in a hurry.' The woman was almost slavering.

'I don't think so. Thanks anyway. There's nothing to stop him just pocketing it is there? And we'd be none the wiser. I'll hang onto it for now and take it to the police station later. I'll phone them while I'm waiting for Lisa so they can reassure the owner if they notice they've dropped it, and get in touch.'

Parked up outside the nursery she counted the money. There was over four thousand pounds in the envelope. Four thousand! What on earth would the owner be thinking when they realised it was lost. Why would anyone carry that much around in cash? She couldn't imagine how she would feel if it happened to her, but then she had never had four thousand pounds lying around to put in an envelope in the first place. Four thousand pounds! Just dropped, loose, apparently from a bag or a pocket. She had never even seen that amount of money before, it made her head spin. She replaced it in the envelope as the first children began to dribble out of the nursery doorway. No time now to phone the police station, she would have to do it from home.

She collected Lisa and went back to the car, desperately hoping that the old mini would start, which, after a few sluggish attempts it did. What a difference four thousand pounds would make to their lives. The dentist could be paid, the car serviced and the MOT. They might even manage a weekend away somewhere – recapture some of the magic. Taken up with the children's tea and homework and Lisa's bedtime, she quite forgot about the money, then glanced at the clock as she heard Anthony's key in the door. Seven o'clock already. She had just put the potatoes on to boil when there was a knock at the front door.

Two uniformed policemen stood there and asked with serious faces whether they could come in.

Vivien felt her face flush and Anthony didn't help, asking 'What is it, officers? What's the matter?'

The older officer looked solemnly at Vivien's face. 'Have you not told your husband about your find this afternoon, Madam?'

'I've not had chance yet,' she burbled, 'he's only just home.'

Embarrassed, although she had done nothing wrong, she blurted out. 'I found some money Anthony. I was going to take it to the police station, but there isn't one in the village and I was going to take it into town once I'd collected Lisa, but she was hungry and then the other children were home and had homework to help with and I didn't get chance.'

Nobody said anything, and Vivien grabbed her bag and rummaged in the front pocket where she had put the envelope. 'Here,' she thrust it at the policeman, 'Take it, take it and give it back to whoever lost it.' She was close to tears now, they all seemed to be looking at her so accusingly.

'How did you track me down?' She meant it as a joke but it made her sound so guilty and of course the policemen wouldn't answer her. Probably that woman had taken her car number as she drove away from the car park. She fancied Anthony was looking at her strangely.

The younger policeman took a small notebook from his pocket and wrote out a receipt after counting out the money, 'Four thousand two hundred pounds, that's correct.' He smiled at Vivien but it didn't make her feel any better. She wanted to shout that of course it was correct, but she had come so close to keeping the money. She had wanted to so badly.

'Would you like us to pass on your details to the owner?' the young policeman asked, 'There might be a reward.'

'Oh no, no, not at all,' she said quickly, 'just make sure it gets back where it belongs. I'm sorry I didn't phone to say I'd got it, I should have done, I was just so busy. I was going to bring it to the police station after taking Lisa to nursery tomorrow, I'm so sorry.'

Smiling now, the two officers left. It was a relief to get rid of the responsibility of the decision of what to do, but she fancied Anthony may never quite look at her in the same way again.

'Ah well,' she said to herself as she served out their meal, 'Of course I would never really have kept the money, but it was nice to dream, if only for a little while.'

The Honeysuckle Tray

For more than ten years Lesley had worked at two jobs and this was her last shift at the homewares factory in Stoke. She had been saving hard, so that she could leave both jobs and go to university to follow her dream of becoming a teacher. The very last item she vacuum-wrapped and packed in the consignment to go off to the warehouse was a square plastic tray, patterned with brightly coloured honeysuckle. It was a pretty pattern but a bit garish for Lesley's taste, otherwise she might have been tempted to liberate it for her own use.

The tray was duly dispatched to the distribution centre, and from there to the big homeware store in town where the assistant liked the pattern so much that she put it in the middle of the front window and made a complete display based on its colours.

Steph bought the square tray thinking it would make a good base to protect the carpet from her Christmas Tree. On Christmas Eve her friend Zoë arrived unannounced and brought Steph a present. In a panic because she had no present to give in return, Steph suggested that her husband take Zoë into the kitchen and pour her a drink. Once alone she snatched the tray and hurried upstairs with it where she wiped it, wrapped it and then brought it down again.

There was an awkward moment as Zoë's eyes strayed to the bottom of the Christmas tree. Evidently she had already noticed the tray, and it was obvious from the shape what was inside the parcel, a tray is a difficult shape to disguise. Opening the tray the next morning Zoë's thoughts were confirmed and she was very hurt. There was even a circular mark from the bottom of the plant pot. That was the beginning of the end of their friendship, and Zoë took the tray to the charity shop during the first week of January.

Gaynor passed the charity shop on her lunch break and thought that the tray would make a lovely Mothers' Day gift for her mum. It looked brand new, still with the label on the bottom. In February she sowed a range of seeds in new pots, and decided to use the tray to move them indoors each night. At the beginning of March she planted out her seedlings, cleaned the tray up and took it round on Mothering Sunday. Her mum made appreciative noises, and served their cups of tea and cake on it. Then, when Gaynor had left, she washed it carefully and tucked it away in the kitchen cupboard because she thought it looked a bit faded and didn't much like it. Anyway she already had several other trays.

When she went to the Mothers' Union meeting the following month, Gaynor's mother used the tray to carry her offering of fairy cakes for the Faith Supper. The idea was that everyone took something; cakes, sandwiches, crisps, whatever. Everybody had something to eat, then took home with them anything left from the food that they had brought Except for Mary. Mary was notorious for taking empty carrier bags to the Faith Suppers and taking home not only any leftovers of her own offerings, but as much food as she could carry in the bags she had brought for exactly that purpose. The other ladies muttered about her for a while each time, but they were used to her doing this on a regular basis. Nobody ever seemed willing to do anything about it. On this occasion she slid the tray into one of her bags along with the food, before wishing everybody goodnight. Gaynor's mother watched her from the other side of the hall but said nothing, she was really quite happy for the tray to go missing in this way.

Mary's granddaughter had an end of year party at school in July. Mary's daughter sent the tray loaded with sandwiches, but her daughter kept forgetting to bring it home, and when the school was deep-cleaned for the summer holidays the tray was stowed away in one of the big kitchen cupboards.

It was there that Irene, one of the cooks found it and made enquiries as to its ownership. All the other trays were grey metal, utilitarian and enormous, except for this one with the honeysuckle pattern. Nobody seemed to know where it had come from. Talking to the supervisor Irene said that she coveted the tray to put on the table beside her mum's chair. It offended Irene's sense of order that there were pills, potions and tissues scattered around the place; it looked untidy. What she didn't say was that she suspected her mum's little table might be an antique, and when she inherited it, she didn't want the top spoiled by scratches and stained with hot tea spillages. The supervisor said that she might as well take it. Irene's mother Edith was delighted and used the tray constantly for nearly three years, until one day, taking it through to the kitchen to be washed, she dropped it. The corner broke off, leaving a brutally sharp edge.

At ninety four years of age, Edith found the recycling rules confusing. The council employees were very good, nobody expected her to drag her bin to the gate. One of the men would come up the drive for it and bring it back, usually with a cheery wave or thumbs up. She worried about the honeysuckle tray. It was evidently made of plastic but she couldn't find the little triangle symbol that she thought meant it could go in the blue bin. After a great deal of worrying, she left it and the broken section propped against the recycling bin with a little note: *Sorry if this is the wrong bin. I wasn't sure. Edith.* The following Tuesday she watched anxiously from the kitchen window. The bin was emptied and when she stepped outside afterwards the tray and the broken sliver had gone.

Ted gave the old lady a cheerful wave and slid the two pieces of broken plastic into the cab of the recycling lorry. It was strictly against the rules, but when they reached the depot he was able to transfer it to his car with nobody any the wiser. At home he used a two-part epoxy to fix the tray and passed it on to Lesley his niece, who was a newly qualified teacher.

'I used to wrap and pack trays like this before I went to university,' she told him. 'When I was saving up so I could afford not to work while I was studying. In fact the very last tray I packed up on my last day's work looked very like this one, only the pattern was much brighter. I always thought it was pretty but a bit garish. I wonder whatever happened to that one.'

The Singletons

I come across all sorts of bits and pieces as I take my daily walks: a jacket hung from the branches of a tree; sometimes, disgustingly, a pair of knickers or men's briefs. But it is the singletons that I feel sorry for and that have always sparked my interest the most.

There were two where I walked yesterday. One had been there for months of course. It was small, purple – although faded now – and made of some rubbery plastic. I first noticed it way back in May, when the weather was warm and getting warmer. It had been in the gutter the first time I saw it. I noticed it but walked on by – it was of little interest to me. The one I saw for the first time yesterday was much more interesting.

The second time I walked past the small one, someone had picked it up and placed it on the wall of the nearest house. It has stood there ever since, getting bleached by the sun and washed by the rain. Now as winter approaches it is clear that it will never be reclaimed. It would be ludicrous to think it would be of any use to the owner now, faded and outgrown as it undoubtedly is.

It's quite easy to explain of course. It's the right size to have been kicked off some small child's foot as they were wheeled along in their buggy. But why would the adult not be aware that it was missing? Wouldn't they retrace their steps when they reached home, or the shops or the house of whoever they had gone to visit? Perhaps they went to catch a bus or a train; perhaps they lived out of the area. Perhaps the sandals were already on the small side and it was not worth the effort of searching. Yes, it was very easily explained.

The one that I saw for the first time yesterday was quite different – an adult shoe, black patent with diamanté bits meant to imitate diamonds all the way up the back and sides, and a smart designer manufacturer's logo on the heel. It was a size 6, my size and I fantasised about wearing it myself. It was a shoe fit for a ball, or for a party, not suitable to walk out along that rough path at all. Perhaps it had been worn to an assignation, something naughty maybe. I would give it some thought.

Today I couldn't take my usual walk of course, all that twisty plastic blue and white tape is in the way, but I know that neither of those shoes will be there. Nor will there be jackets, underwear, nor the more mundane empty coke bottles and crisp packets. The whole route will have been picked clean and everything will have been closely examined, except for the single black shoe.

I've been told to wait at home, not to leave the house until the police have been and talked to me. I wonder if I will be able to leave the house once they've finished, or maybe I'll be made to leave the house.

I suppose I'll have to tell them. They told me that someone saw me pick up the black shoe and put it in my bag. They told me that there's no point trying to get rid of it – they'll be here in ten minutes and they want to examine it for something called DNA.

I shall have to decide what to say, and I'm not very good at lying. I'll tell them I found it yesterday, which is true, but do I also need to tell them that while, strictly speaking that was the first time I had seen it, I'd previously seen its facsimile – nice word, I must remember that in a photograph in my husband's wallet, a photograph of the other woman.

Will I have to tell them that because of that photograph I took to following them and spying on them when they met, the most recent time being two evenings ago, when he was "working late at the office"? (How gullible does he think I am?) but really meeting her for some assignation. "Look good," he had told her in his text – "wear the black with the sparkly shoes."

I wonder where he was planning to take her. They never got there of course. She had a mishap shall we say, en route to their rendezvous. Perhaps I'll find out eventually what his plans were for that evening – maybe he'll have to say it in court.

And of course I'll be there in the court. Oh yes, I'll be there.

The Magic Decorations

Hazel could not understand the attraction of her daughter Fiona's new boyfriend. She just hadn't taken to him. Fiona had known Kyle such a short time and now he had moved into her Manchester flat. The flat was just down the road from where Hazel's ex-husband, Fiona's father lived.

'Kyle's had a tough life, Mum. I never realised that parents could treat their child like he was treated.'

So he said.

'But surely sympathy's no basis for a relationship, Fee.'

When the phone call ended Hazel had tried to push the uncharitable thoughts out of her head. There had been a distinct coolness in Fiona's invitation to visit her and Kyle over Christmas, but she very much wanted to spend time with her daughter.

Case already packed, and presents loaded in the car, Hazel called at her sister's for some tea and sympathy. Now she sat tearfully while her sister told her that she must try and get over this wariness. It was not what Hazel wanted to hear.

'You'll have to Hazel, otherwise you'll lose her.'

'What do you mean?'

'If you're not nice to him, you'll force Fiona to choose. She's in love, she'll choose him. Now,' she picked up Hazel's little dog, 'leave this gorgeous little chap to enjoy Christmas with his Aunty, and go and see your daughter.'

Hazel had had mixed feelings about her daughter's invitation to stay over Christmas. Whilst she dearly loved Fee, it was with a heavy heart that, laden with presents and wine she had locked up carefully and headed up the M6 that afternoon.

Her first thought when Fiona opened the door was how tired her daughter looked, eyes smudged with dark shadows and her hair uncharacteristically lank. Following her into the living room she smiled at Kyle who was lounging on the sofa in front of a television programme, but she was immediately aware of a coolness between him and her daughter. Kyle took his time turning off the television and smiling at Hazel.

'At last,' he drawled, though Hazel had arrived at the appointed time, 'Now we can eat. I'm starving.' With a quick movement he leapt to his feet and looked meaningfully at Fiona.

'Lovely,' she said, tucking a stray lock of hair behind her ear. 'It's all ready.'

Hazel left her bags by the sofa where Kyle ignored them, and she followed Fiona into the kitchen.

'What can I do to help?' she asked, more brightly than she felt. Fiona paused in lifting a casserole dish from the oven.

'Oh,' she said, 'there's wine in the fridge and some beer for Kyle.'

Hazel ventured, 'Are you okay, Fee? You seem tired.'

'I'm fine, Mum, just busy at work. You know it's our busiest time, the run-up to Christmas.' She spoke sharply and Hazel smoothly changed the conversation to Christmas plans. Fiona took the casserole to the table and sat back in her chair.

'I finished work today though, so now I can relax.' She gave her mother a strained smile.

The atmosphere was palpable throughout the meal, and Hazel worked hard to keep the conversation going. This was going to be a difficult few days. Kyle was even more taciturn than usual, and she noticed that her daughter ate very little and drank hardly anything. She had always been slim but she seemed thinner than ever.

After the table was cleared away, Hazel helped wash up and was just hanging up the tea towel when Kyle appeared in the doorway.

'I'm off to the pub, are you coming girls?'

Hazel took her cue from her daughter who was shaking her head.

'I think I'll stay and chat to Fiona,' she told him, 'We don't get chance very often.'

Fiona looked relieved, and the two settled down in the small living room but Hazel found it difficult to say any of the things she really wanted to. As the conversation dwindled to nothing the younger woman dozed off on the sofa and Hazel took the opportunity to take her bags into the spare room. Waking Fiona gently with a cup of tea at ten o'clock she seized her chance before Kyle returned.

'Fiona, tea,' she said. As her daughter rubbed her neck and stretched, she ploughed on, 'Darling I don't want to interfere, but is everything really all right? You look so tired tonight.' The younger woman gathered her thoughts for a minute, then, 'No, I told you Mum, everything's fine. I've just been busy that's all.'

Before Hazel had a chance to press further, the door banged and Kyle came in on a waft of beer and cigarette smoke.

'Well, girls,' he said, more expansive and red-cheeked through drink, 'have you put the world to rights?'

When Fiona made no reply he went and leaned over her to give her a kiss. She flinched from the beer breath and Kyle turned away impatiently.

'Have you told your mum our news?' he said, head on one side, his tone saying more than his words. Fiona exhaled deeply.

'No,' she said sharply, 'We said we weren't telling anyone just yet.'

'Oh, but your mum? Surely you've told your mum?' He turned his back so that he was facing Hazel. 'How do you fancy being a granny?' he asked, 'Fiona has got herself pregnant.'

Hazel glanced across at her daughter, who was looking at her in some trepidation.

'It's true, Mum,' she said in a bright, false voice. 'We just found out, and it's very early days. We weren't going to tell anyone just yet, but,' she reached for Kyle's reluctant hand, 'you're different. Kyle's right. You should know straight away. Of course we're delighted,' she finished lamely.

Hazel looked from one to the other. Kyle looked anything but delighted, and Fiona was watching her anxiously.

'Well, congratulations to you both,' she said, hoping she sounded more enthusiastic than she felt. 'By next Christmas you'll have a family of your own. Of course I see now why you went easy on the wine.'

'We should celebrate now,' said Kyle, heading for the fridge, 'Red or white, Hazel?' as he got himself another beer.

'Oh, no thanks, Kyle, I won't be able to sleep if I have more to drink now. I'll just rinse these mugs and then head to bed if that's okay. We have plenty of time to celebrate over the next few days.'

Fiona looked at her gratefully, 'I'm heading for bed too. Goodnight Mum.'

*   *   *

Later, unable to sleep for all the thoughts crowding into her head, Hazel could not avoid hearing the conversation from the next room. These were not the intimate sounds of endearment, but rather harsh words spoken low so as not to disturb her. She heard Kyle say, in response to a comment from Fiona, 'She'd have wormed it out of you. Mothers are like that.'

'Well, will we? Get married I mean.'

'Let's not rush our fences. I've got to get used to the idea of being a dad first.'

Hazel wanted to be privy to none of this. She tried to ignore it and compose herself for sleep, but through the thin walls she could not shut it out, just as she could not fail to notice the negative tone to Kyle's

133

responses. She lay wakeful long after the voices had silenced, hearing a clock somewhere nearby striking three.

The next day conversation was difficult with Kyle there. There was so much Hazel wanted to ask Fiona, but since Kyle came in from the pub the previous evening there had been no opportunity. Now that her daughter had finished work for the holiday she hoped that they would be able to have a proper talk. As the time progressed however, it seemed more and more unlikely. Fiona was very evidently avoiding a heart-to-heart, and seemed to find Kyle's conversation over-funny and very clever.

Hazel tried to think of the best outcome to the present situation and failed to come up with anything that seemed acceptable. She toyed momentarily with the prospect of giving up her job and offering to mind the child, but what would Kyle be doing meantime. He showed no signs of looking for work, and seemed quite content to live off his girlfriend's earnings.

During the morning Hazel desperately fished around for a topic to talk about, which wouldn't involve families, parenthood or jobs and income. In the end she partially succeeded. To her daughter she said, 'I've brought you the Magic Decorations.'

'The what?' Kyle looked bewildered

Despite herself Hazel smiled. 'Well, the Magic Decorations. I brought them for Fiona,' the pause was momentary, 'and you too of course.' Seeing his quizzical expression she sat back to tell the tale.

'It's a sort of family tradition now. When I was little my nan took me each December to a Manchester store to see Father Christmas, usually in Lewis's, or Kendal's in more affluent times. Eventually of course every garden centre had a Santa. Anyway we always went out for lunch afterwards and I was allowed to choose a tree decoration each year. Unbeknown to me, each year Nan made a note of the year, a description of what I had chosen, where it had come from, and so on. Then later she added a few more points about that Christmas itself – what presents I had received and other things that may help me remember it specifically. She stuck them all in a book along with a photograph or two from that year as reminders. Fiona's dad and I were married in December, and that year Nan handed over the whole lot to me, the decorations and the information.

'I kept on the tradition with Fiona, it seemed such a nice idea. Once she set up a home of her own I decided to pass them on to her at this visit. The time seemed right, and now you tell me that by this time next year you will have a youngster of your own.'

Fiona's eyes were teary. 'That's lovely, thanks Mum.'

'Yeah,' said Kyle, before checking again that neither of them wanted to go out to the pub with him.

It seemed to prophecy what Fiona's future life would be.

* * *

Fiona visited her mother in late January, arriving unexpectedly in the middle of the afternoon when Hazel had been sitting in the cosy living room with the dog. The weather was closing in, the sky leaden with unshed snow. The festive lights that had illuminated the village had all been packed away for another year. Hazel had lit the fire, and she hurried her daughter into the warmth.

And Kyle?' Hazel said lightly, looking out of the front window. 'Is he joining us?'

Fiona paused, then sighed deeply, 'Oh Mum, you're so diplomatic. He says that spending the weekend with two old biddies, miles from his mates isn't his idea of fun. I suppose he has a point.'

Hazel wondered what made Fiona an old biddy, and Kyle had originated from the Potteries, surely he had friends around here still. However, she kept her counsel and changed the subject.

'If it's okay with you, I'll stay till Sunday, and see where we go from there.'

It seemed a strange way to put it, but Hazel decided not to pursue that thought for the moment.

The two shared a companionable meal of beef casserole with red wine, followed by Wensleydale cheese and the last of the Christmas cake, their favourite. They had settled down before the fire with the dogs when Fiona's mobile phone rang.

'Hi Kyle. Is everything all right? Oh sweetheart I told you. Probably till Sunday, I said. Yes. Yes. Kyle how much have you had to drink? Kyle! Kyle!'

The connection had been cut. Hazel picked up her knitting.

'They say, don't they, that early pregnancy is one of the most stressful times for relationships?' Fiona seemed not to require an answer. The ache of longing and the humiliation vied for dominance in her voice.

'Is everything all right?' Hazel ventured at last.

'Oh Mum, you know it isn't, but we'll work through it. It's difficult for Kyle.'

Hazel kept her thoughts to herself. She found

she was becoming an expert in diplomacy.

'What are you knitting?' Fiona had turned on the television to a programme of carols, and they watched companionably.

'It's a baby coat, I thought … her voice petered out. 'It will come in handy,' she finished more strongly.

Fiona picked up the pattern, 'That's gorgeous.'

'I find it relaxing. I've always enjoyed knitting, although …' the dog snuggled closer to her on the sofa, 'it is quite difficult with this little one under my arm.'

As the television programme finished she reluctantly put the knitting away.

*   *   *

It was a mere two weeks before Fiona once again arrived at her mother's cottage.

'Mum can I stay, for a while?' Absentmindedly she swept the dog into her arms.

'Of course Fee darling, you know you're always welcome, I've been trying to ring you.' Hazel got to her feet, 'I'll open the radiator, and make up the bed for you.'

'Leave the bed for now, Mum,' Fiona remained seated. 'I have to tell you I've been sort of ill. The reason you couldn't get hold of me was because I've been in hospital,' her eyes filled with tears. 'I've lost the baby, Mum. When I came out your messages were waiting for me.'

'But why didn't Kyle...?' Hazel began, wondering why he had not relayed the message to her the previous day.

'Kyle's gone, Mum. When I was told I could come home from hospital I phoned him, but he didn't pick up, so I got a taxi, and a lot of his stuff had gone, clothes and stuff.

'Oh Fee, I'm so sorry. How do you feel about that?' Hazel was gentle.

Fiona considered. She could think of it now, not without sadness, but without her emotions escaping aloud.

'I'm not sure to be honest. At the moment I'm very emotional, so I'm not really thinking straight. I'm hoping I'll come to see it as a blessing, the miscarriage I mean, and hope that Kyle will come back. Maybe it was just fatherhood that scared him. Oh I don't know.' She shook her head, 'Our disappointment in each other was pretty much mutual recently.'

'Of course you can stay here, as long as you like. But I insist that we make the bed up now, open the radiator to warm that bedroom through, and that you go up for a lie down. You're only just out of hospital, and you've had a real shock coming back to an empty flat. Now, up you go, no arguing.' Hazel was firm.

Fiona slept through till nearly four in the afternoon. Hazel returned from taking the dog around the block to hear her on the phone. It was evidently Kyle on the line, and Hazel went into the kitchen, discreetly closing the door behind her. After a few moments Fiona went through to the kitchen, gathering up her keys and bag.

'Kyle wants to talk, Mum. He's just got back to the flat. I'm going to go up and see him. I owe him that.'

Hazel privately thought that Fiona owed Kyle nothing, but remained noncommittal. She was aware that, as Kyle had gone, so he might come back, in which case anything negative she said would be wrong in the context of their future relationship. In view of Fiona just having left hospital she merely said: 'I think you'd be more sensible to leave it until tomorrow, but if you're determined to go now, then please go carefully, and ring me if you need anything, oh and here, take my spare front door key, then you can let yourself in here anytime.

*   *   *

It was gone midnight when Hazel heard the front door close again. The dog raised his head, and wagged his tail as Fiona came in. She looked crushed, devastated. Over cups of hot chocolate in front of the fire, she told Hazel about it. Kyle was so relieved that they had lost the baby, but said that they would carry on as before, as long as she would promise not to get pregnant again.

All sorts of unkind things were said on both sides, and she had told him that she thought they should separate, at least for a while, so they could get their feelings sorted out. She asked where he had been staying, and he flew into a rage. She wasn't his keeper, he could stay where he wanted to, and so on. She said she thought that he had better leave, and he was delighted. He told her he was going to pull some bird who wouldn't saddle him with a kid at the first opportunity. But then he said he loved her, and refused to go.

'Then he threw a plate at me. I was really quite

scared, and just walked out and left him there, in my flat! What a fool I've been, Mum. Thank goodness I didn't end up having his baby. He's been rough with me before, but this... I could hear him breaking stuff as I left. I'll have to go back tomorrow, if only to get the rest of my stuff but...' She broke down in tears.

'I tell you what might be better,' Hazel suggested, handing her the tissues and stroking her hair. 'Call your dad tomorrow morning, he's on the spot – tell him to get the locks changed as soon as possible. If there's any argument from a locksmith, he can call you for permission. Then you can go up, and see what's what when you're ready.'

Fiona hesitated. 'I don't want dad to know what a mess I'm making of my life.'

'Your dad is in no position to criticise anyone's lifestyle. Come to that, nobody should criticise your lifestyle. If you are happy, that's all that matters, and you won't be happy till you get this sorted.' Hazel was brisk. 'Phone your dad first thing tomorrow.'

*   *   *

It was later the next day when Fiona drove to her father's house to collect her new keys, and then on to her flat to collect the rest of her things. Her father offered to accompany her but she declined.

'It's a mess, my love,' he persisted, 'Kyle must have been back before you asked me to change the locks. There have been some breakages.' It was a mastery of understatement.

'No Dad. Thanks, but I want to go on my own.'

As soon as she opened the door she faced the turmoil, and was grateful that her father had been

140

persuaded not to come back with her. It seemed right that having got herself into this mess, it should be up to her to deal with the fallout. And what a vindictive mess it was.

Every breakable item in the kitchen had been thrown on the floor. Books had been ripped and soaked in a bath half-filled apparently for just this purpose. She could not believe the venom with which the attack had been carried out. Her clothes were shredded in the wardrobes, left shoes were soaking and ruined in the bath, the right one of each pair uselessly safe in the cupboard.

In the living room she stared amazed. Nothing was touched or damaged in here except for the Magic Decorations, the box of which had been removed from its storage place in the spare bedroom.

Each piece had been individually unwrapped and smashed. There were fragments of coloured glass and metal pulverised into the carpet, as if the heel of a boot had deliberately been used to grind them in. Suddenly in the corner, something caught Fiona's eye, it was one decoration that must have rolled under the chair to safety.

Unwrapping the bauble, she found it was the one bought when she was tiny. *Baby's First Christmas,* very faded now, was etched across its surface. It was too much for Fiona, and she sat and sobbed.

Eventually she pulled herself together and was looking through the Yellow Pages for someone to clear away the shambles when the phone rang. Her dad.

'Are you okay, my love?'

'Yes Dad, I'll be fine. I'm just relieved that I've

got out of this relationship now. He's one very sick man.'

'What are you going to do? I can come over right now, and help if you like – I don't want to interfere, but it might be easier. I'd like to help.'

'Oh, yes please, Dad. I'm feeling a bit fragile and this has knocked me for six. I'm going to give up the lease on the flat and get this lot cleared. I'll be staying with Mum for the moment.'

When they had finished packing up what was essential, including the treasured Christmas bauble, Fiona's father looked around the devastation.

'Do you want me to deal with this lot for you? I will, you know. It's easier for me being on the spot than you hiking up and down the motorway.' Her father could be remarkably perspicacious, 'That way you needn't come back to the flat ever if you don't want to. I can parcel up anything retrievable, and send it on or bring it down to you.'

Suddenly chilled by the unpleasantness of the situation, Fiona told him that she'd be grateful. She would load her car with what they had managed to salvage, and he could send on anything else.

'I don't want to come back to the flat if I can avoid it. I want to draw a line under all this, and move on with my life.'

She had been relieved that her father had never been told about the baby, she had felt it would have diminished her in his eyes.

Back in the little bedroom at Hazel's Fiona unwrapped the sole surviving Christmas decoration, and consoled herself that one day, when the time was right, she would have a tree of her own to hang it on, along perhaps with a baby of her own, for whom she could kick-start the tradition of the Magic Decorations.

Honeymoon Tales

(1)   Tanks for the Memory

It could have been one of the shortest honeymoons, one of the shortest marriages, ever.

A romantic week in the Yorkshire Dales, with all the usual tourist places to visit – York, Richmond, Helmsley and so on.

I had no idea, although my new husband did, that there is an army barracks based nearby. I'd heard of Catterick, who hasn't? But I had no idea where it was, nor that it was an army training base. I can't say, to be honest, that I'd given it much thought at all, it was just a name that came up on the television from time to time.

This particular morning we had decided to head out into the countryside. We were staying near Thirsk and were heading for Richmond, which we had been told was particularly picturesque.

At the time the car we were driving was a small yellow Vauxhall, not that it matters what we were driving really, we were always going to be at a disadvantage. For as we rounded a bend in one of the country lanes edged with tall hedgerows, a most peculiar sight appeared, the like of which I have never seen before or since on the public roads.

It was a tank, I didn't know at the time what make or model, although I was later told it was a Chieftain. My mind absorbed only that it was a tank, and a few details. It was adorned with two L-plates, it was absolutely enormous, it was coming at some speed towards us round the bend in the road, and it was travelling backwards.

If a photograph of our expressions could have been taken at that second it would have been worth a fortune on social media or television bloopers programmes. What went through my mind? Only that those things can't half move whatever direction they're facing in. I suppose we were fortunate that it wasn't going forwards, otherwise with its massive gun pointing at us it would probably have looked even more intimidating. As it was there was no way we could outrun it, and to do a three-point turn in that little lane would have taken ages. There was absolutely no evasive action we could take.

After what seemed like a lifetime it slewed to a halt. Somebody in military uniform got out of what I can only describe as the passenger side. He raised his hand in apology, and he looked furious. I presume whoever had been in the driving seat – I'm guessing now, I have no idea of the layout of the inside of a tank, funnily enough it's not been something I've ever thought might be useful to know – had slid across out of the way as our guy climbed up on the driver's side. The tank was driven off, forwards thankfully, and turned into the first opening so that we could pass.

We have been married fifty years this year so what could have been the shortest honeymoon ever didn't do us any harm. My husband, a master baker, has just produced the cake for the party to celebrate our anniversary – a beautiful replica of a Chieftain tank, complete with L plates.

I can only hope that poor learner driver didn't get into too much trouble. I wonder whether he has any idea how much hilarity he has provided us with ever since, every time we see a tank.

Honeymoon Tales

(2)   Oil Drums

I had never entered a competition before, but the one in this magazine seemed ideal, and I entered it in good faith.

Tell us about your holiday disasters it read, *We'll pay £200 for every article we print.*

I thought we were a shoe-in for winning £200, especially as the holiday in question had been our honeymoon.

There had been a letter of notification and, had we been more worldly-wise, we may have understood sooner what had happened.
This was the early nineteen seventies remember, ATOL protection was non-existent as yet,

and the letter didn't worry us particularly. In fact, the prospect of a refund of ten pounds for each of us, off the total honeymoon cost of £86 was cause for delight. As was the voucher for a free meal for two at one of the many restaurants in the resort.

These sweeteners arrived with the letter just three days before the wedding, and the honeymoon flight to Spain was scheduled for the day after the ceremony. The wording of the letter was peculiar, which perhaps should have alerted us, but this was to be our first time abroad, and we knew nothing.

It was headed Clarkson's – a name you probably won't be familiar with unless you are of a certain age. It was, at that time, one of the biggest tour operators selling holidays on the Spanish coast and in the Balearics. The company spectacularly went bust in 1972. It was a huge concern, and it was the first time that a travel company of this importance had gone under. Guess what year we got married! You can see where this is going can't you?

The brochure we had booked from many months previously had not shown a photograph of the hotel we were booked into, but a very attractive *Artist's Impression.* This was fairly commonplace at the time, with hotels being built incredibly quickly across the Costas to fulfil the dreams of sun-starved Brits.

This letter now told us that the hotel had unavoidably had to be built five miles outside of the resort, instead of centrally as had originally been advertised; hence the compensation offered. There would also be a regular free shuttle bus service into the town.

And this was the letter that arrived just four days before we were due to fly. It seemed amazing that only at this late stage the company chose to notify us that the hotel was built somewhere else. It seemed we had no choice but to go along with it or lose our much anticipated, and fully paid-for, honeymoon altogether.

When we arrived it was evident that much of the letter was a lie, or at least creative with the truth. The hotel where we were deposited was very clearly brand-new. So new that it wasn't even finished. There was a lot of wet plaster and no pool. There was no kitchen, and no proper terrace, just a pile of rubble.

It was not called the Hotel Miramar at all. It was called the Caesar II. Immediately across the road, fronting onto the beach was the Hotel Caesar, and we were being housed in what was obviously an annex to this prestigious edifice. There was no tour representative to whom we could have complained, and the tour rep at the Hotel Caesar was clearly not interested. It transpired that as an emergency measure their new not-yet-ready-for-occupancy annex had been given over to us, the Clarkson's travellers, who may otherwise have been sleeping on the beach. That was as far as their responsibility went.

Our food was cooked in the Caesar kitchens and carried across the road to the Caesar II dining room where we ate it cold. Our waitress was able to tell us that she had been employed the day before arrived, she had never worked in a hotel before, that much was evident, and that all the staff were only contracted to work for three weeks.

We were due to stay for ten days and on the

second day we got the regular free shuttle bus, which travelled just once a day albeit at a regular time, into the town. The place where our hotel should have been built was a car park, with no indication that this situation had ever been destined to change, interesting. On day three the rain began. The following morning a group of us gathered round the public telephone in the Hotel Caesar's foyer, whilst one of our fellow travellers phoned the airport to see if we could get an earlier flight home. One set of holidaymakers were due to fly home that day anyway but we couldn't. The flights were fully booked. We were stuck on the sunshine coast in the rain.

That evening as the rains continued the water level had risen alarmingly. This of course was no fault of the tour operator, except that our hotel shouldn't have been there in the first place. By the evening it was evident that there was serious trouble. Several holidaymakers, including my new husband, fell ill with a tummy bug. You really don't want to know the details, suffice to say it was very unpleasant. Then to add insult to injury, with the annex now less than half occupied, the water supply to the Caesar II was turned off.

We were told that it was because of the floods – problems with the drains. There were certainly problems with the drains, we could all smell it! We would be moved across the road to the neighbouring hotel we were told. And so it was that a series of oil drums with planks across was placed across the road for us to cross over this now significant river. Our luggage was scooped up in the shovel of a digger and lifted high in the air while the vehicle crossed over to the Hotel Caesar's front door on its massive wheels.

We staggered across the planks with staff wading alongside to help us, half of us carrying handbags and several still carrying sick bags.

The honeymoon did improve from there on in, with the Caesar staff at least trained to wait on at the tables. There was a swimming pool with water and a terrace on which to laze. The rain stopped and the health problems sorted themselves out in a matter of twenty-four hours too. With proper clean water and, ignoring the first half of the venture, we were able to honestly say when people asked that we had enjoyed our honeymoon.

And now a reply had come in response to my magazine submission. Very excited I opened the letter, another letter that didn't give me the message I wanted:

Sorry we are unable to use your submission at this time, they had written, *We find that our readers like an element of realism in our stories and there are just too many unbelievable coincidences in your narrative. We hope you will carry on writing fiction and wish you success with future submissions.*

Huh! Too many unbelievable coincidences indeed! Writing fiction! How could that possibly be the case when every word I had written was true?

Hiawatha

Tina woke with a jolt, her head pounding along with her heart. Gradually wakefulness brought her back to reality and her heart slowed. Consciously she breathed deeply – there was no need for concern. Everything was on track as it should be. The school performance of Hiawatha was only a week away and the girls had rehearsed it to death. Each family had been tasked with buying their daughter's costume from the same outfitters in town. The birds' costumes – yes there are birds in Hiawatha, who knew? – were a simple filmy garment in a nondescript beige colour. It came along with a bag of feathers that were to be attached to it by hand.

The only thing required of her in readiness for the production was the organisation of the dress for her daughter Leah. The dress had been collected and an alteration was needed – a simple job even for someone of Tina's needlework experience. As she drank her morning tea she reflected back on what she thought of as *the saga of the dresses.*

It had begun weeks ago with an initial note from the school. The play was to be performed for five nights in December at the local Garrick theatre in town, and it was an honour to have been chosen to take part – especially for Year Seven students, who had only started at the school in September. Only eight girls had been chosen from the whole year and they were to dance as birds. Leah was one of them.

The note had gone on to say that the school was trying to minimise expense, and they hoped that each girl's parents would be able to provide their own costume, and take on some minor alterations if needed. There was a fund to help parents who would be challenged to meet the costs, but Tina would have died rather than admit that she could have done with that sort of help.

If she was honest Tina was sick of Leah's continuous dancing around the house, to her own tuneless rendition of the music. She also wasn't sure about five whole nights ferrying her daughter into town in the dark winter evenings, then home late for five consecutive nights in the run-up to Christmas, but it would have been churlish to say so. It was far too late to back out now anyway. It would mess up the whole production. The dress had been bought, a creation of voile over sateen, and thankfully the birds would be barefoot, as of course birds are, so shoes were not an issue.

* * *

The dress for Leah had been bought in November. This was a very popular outfitters in the area and goods were snapped up quickly. The teachers had suggested early purchase of all the costumes to avoid any difficulties.

At the beginning of December Leah had tried her dress on again. She wanted her visiting Grandma to see it when she came to stay, and it was then, in the cold winter daylight that Tina noticed the problem – the problem that they had all missed in the shop. Down the back of the dress, because the zip had been poorly fitted, a thread was pulled from waistline to hem. Under the lights, as they danced and twirled, everyone would be able to see the fault and wonder why she had not spotted it before.

She contacted the retailer's help-line, speaking to a helpful lady who explained patiently that this was part of their summer line, they had sold out on account of a production by the local high school, and that it was no longer available in the run-up to Christmas. She suggested that some of their other branches may have old stock and that Tina should ring round and find out. Regrettably nothing could be done now about a refund, because of the time lapse, and Tina not keeping the receipt.

She didn't care about the money – she cared about the dress. It had to be right for the forthcoming production, that was all that counted. It was two weeks before Christmas, the shops had other priorities, but eventually after hours of phoning different branches, she tracked down an alternative. Yes, they would check the zip while she was on the phone; yes, the stitching seemed to be perfect; no, there were no flaws in the fabric, Madam. The dress was perfect. The only challenge was that it was an hour's drive away in Edinburgh. It didn't matter – Tina was wholly committed to this production and would do anything to make Leah's week perfect. She took the day off work and went to collect the dress. As the sales assistant had promised, the dress was perfect. The only difficulty was that it was a size larger than Leah needed.

Never mind, Tina would drag the little-used Singer out of its cupboard. A few tucks and it would be fine, especially with strategically placed feathers.

*   *   *

She lugged the old sewing machine onto the table and plugged it in. She was no needlework novice but the shiny sateen and voile had a tendency to slide about, making tacking essential and time-consuming. It was while she sat to one side of the machine, tacking the newly-positioned shoulder seams, that the sewing machine suddenly began to stitch of its own accord. With no fabric under the pressure foot and nobody within touching distance the light suddenly turned on, the motor whirred and the needle moved furiously like some kind of demented ghost.

Tina burst out laughing, it looked so comical, but then she smelled the hot, electrical smell and saw a tiny whiff of smoke rising from the foot control. Quick as a flash she flicked the switch off on the wall, cutting the power, as the smoke firstly grew into a steady stream then subsided. Now what could she do? She needed to get these alterations completed in the next twenty four hours.

It was three o'clock on the Monday morning when she at last put down the needle. The alterations were complete, all done by hand. With both layers to be done, and the side seams as well as the shoulders to be taken in; then the feathers to be attached, it had been quite a task. Hanging the dress up on the doorframe she dragged herself up to bed. There had been just the one chance to get this right. Opening night was tomorrow – tonight now – and she had just breakfast time before school to try the dress on Leah and hope that it fitted. The dress rehearsal was this afternoon and all the girls had to take their outfits to school this morning.

The seven o'clock alarm dragged her up from the depths of sleep and with fingers crossed she helped Leah shower and try on the dress. It was perfect! Thankfully she dispatched Leah and the dress to the care of her teacher.

Struggling to stay awake that evening she went to support Leah in the first of the five performances. She was delighted to see as the little birds came dancing onto the stage that Leah's dress fitted as well as any. She breathed out a massive sigh of relief and settled back to enjoy the performance.

The Cropredy Lectern

I know it had been my dad's dream for years to own his own canal boat; not a big fancy narrow boat, just something modest, and eventually he bought a day boat, not even five metres long, which he lovingly overhauled, adding an awning and a cooking space. He even managed to squeeze in sleeping accommodation for the three of us, with me sleeping with my feet in the gas cylinder cupboard.

I think the problem for me was that when you're about thirteen or fourteen years old you want to be out and about with friends, not cruising down the canals at snails' pace. I was too young to be left to my own devices while my parents went off on the boat, and so perforce I was dragged along too. At least that was how I saw it; dragged along at a maximum speed of four knots.

I remember the first weekend we took the boat out. We collected it from where it was moored early on the Saturday morning, returning to the same place late the following evening. I checked the road map afterwards, to find that the furthest point we actually visited on that journey could have been reached in just over half an hour by car.

At least that first journey had the advantage in that the weather was glorious. Sitting on top of the boat watching the world go by had a special sort of charm, especially in the rural bits of the journey. Not every outing was so clement. In heavy rain we were necessarily bundled together in the cabin, or walking the towpath getting soaked, with nowhere to dry wet clothes. If you chose to walk there were times when you had to wait for the boat to catch up! Yes, really, in whatever the weather was throwing at you. So you can see I was not particularly a fan.

There were other issues for me as well. For example I had no idea that I had such a fear of heights until one holiday when our little boat ricocheted drunkenly across the Pontcysyllte Aqueduct in North Wales. No amount of coaxing could get me back on that boat for the return journey, and I walked across the towpath, grimly hanging onto the handrail.

There were some good points about boating though. It was on the boat that I saw my very first kingfisher, but the best and most memorable incident for me was, I suppose with hindsight, a bit of an expensive disaster for my parents. We were travelling south along the Oxford Canal, when the outboard motor hit something underwater, and needed repairs that were beyond my dad's capability. We were fortunate in that someone based at the nearby Cropredy Marina would be able to carry out the repair, but we would have an unscheduled stop of twenty-four hours while he acquired the necessary spare parts and completed the job.

The nature of canal boating is such that, whether the boat is hired or is your own, you generally need to end your holiday or weekend or overnight stop back where you started, that is wherever you left your car, and so unwanted pit stops like this are not generally a good idea. It is also the case that if you are stranded like we were, you were necessarily stranded with no transport at all. There was no choice in this case. Either we took twenty four hours in the environs of Cropredy, or we stayed there stranded forever.

Cropredy is a small village, best-known nowadays for its long-established music festival, but this story predates the festival days by many decades and there seriously was not a lot to do. Wandering around the churchyard of the beautiful Church of St Mary the Virgin, we met the then-incumbent, whose name I don't now recall. He gave us a tour of the eleventh century church and fascinating it was.

Scroll back a few centuries and Cropredy was very interesting. Situated on the river Cherwell, just a few miles south of Banbury, the village was the site of a major battle during the English Civil War in 1644. The Battle of Cropredy Bridge is well-documented and was key to the outcome of the war. In advance of the battle, it was decided to hide the church's most precious artefacts in case the Parliamentarians won, in which case these would almost certainly be destroyed.

There was of course no canal in Cropredy then, but the bridge in question crossed over the River Cherwell and these artefacts, including the tripedal brass lectern, were hidden in the river itself for safekeeping, within metres of where the battle took place.

It was the lectern's story that I remember so clearly. The lectern, majestically topped with its symbolic eagle, was not recovered from the river for some fifty years. Nobody seems to have recorded why it took so long, but by that time it was completely black and one of its three claw feet was missing.

Believing the lectern to be made of iron, a new foot was commissioned and forged by the local blacksmith, and it was only after this new foot was fitted that some particularly enthusiastic cleaning revealed that the lectern itself was in fact made of solid brass.

There was discussion about whether a new, matching foot should be created, but it was decided to leave the lectern as it now was, and to this day, the lectern can be seen in the church, standing on its three mismatched feet.

To me it seems to be a timely reminder that long after those involved in both sides of a war are dead and gone, there have also been beautiful and historic buildings and artefacts destroyed, that can never be built back as they were. I hope all the locals are aware of the story and the stark reminder of all the beautiful things that are the victims of wars.

Tom and Jerry

Tom looked down proudly at the bunch of keys in his hand and smiled, his own home at last. To be fair he acknowledged that he had been very fortunate compared with other millennials he knew. Most of them had not yet been in a position to put together the deposit on a tiny terraced house like this one in Willesden, enabling him to move out of the family home.

The house was a mess he had to admit. It had been owned, like many in this area, by a private landlord who had taken over a sitting tenant about a million years ago and had then spent the minimum on it, refusing to do repairs and updating other than the basics required by law. The building society had withheld several thousands of pounds from their loan offer to Tom as the house was not, in their estimation, currently habitable. It was only a bequest in his Aunty Brenda's will that had enabled Tom to make up the shortfall until they were prepared to release the funds.

There had been what the surveyor described as *some rodent activity* in the kitchen, the front of an old sink unit thoroughly chewed by rats just above ground level, and the rest of the house, although sound, was in a pretty rough state.

Tom threw the keys in the air and caught them a couple of times. He didn't care. He would put in the time needed to bring this house back to being a home again. He had some favours to call in, one from his friend's dad who was a plumber. Even as Tom stood looking around he could hear the van arrive bringing the first workman to start what would become a long haul.

Tom's dog Rebel, was sniffing every corner of the house, making himself at home. As long as he had his bed, food and Tom nearby he would settle anywhere. Tom threw the keys on Aunty Brenda's old dining room table and carried on bringing stuff in from his car.

His mum and dad were upstairs, making up his bed and cleaning the bathroom while he carried the two sacks of Rebel's food and treats up into the spare room. If there was a chance that any rats were still around, he wanted them out of the way. At the weekend he would buy a couple of feed bins, the better to store them. Leaving his parents to it, he went downstairs and out of the back door. Rebel would need to learn where it was acceptable to use as a toilet, although the tiny back garden was such a mess it wouldn't really matter. There was a home-made shed, a lean-to Tom supposed it would be called, but it was empty and so rickety that when he opened the door and leaned on the side panel, it collapsed in a heap.

Perhaps he should keep the wood for the wood burner he planned.

*   *   *

Eventually, after a fish and chip supper, his parents left for home, promising to return at the weekend. Thank goodness for Aunty Brenda. The local charity shop had offered his cousin twenty pounds for all the stuff in her house. He had counter-offered fifty and helped his cousin to clear the stuff that nobody wanted to the refuse tip. It meant that his new home was furnished after a fashion. The three piece suite fitted in the tiny front room, just. The kitchen utensils would come in handy and he had bought himself a new bed. By two o'clock in the morning the place didn't exactly look homely, but he had running water – hot and cold, a bed to sleep in and an ancient fridge to store a bit of milk and butter.

Rolling into bed at last, his head hardly seemed to have hit the pillow before he heard unaccountable noises. He was too tired to think clearly, and put it down to his neighbours. Tom had never before lived in anything other than his parents' detached houses through the years, so sharing a party wall was a novelty. Whether it was to become a problem for him or not, remained to be seen.

Woken by a hungry dog long after his usual time, he forgot about the noise, but the following night it happened again. It wasn't a scratching, or music, or footsteps, but it seemed to come from the area of the stairs. He guessed correctly that the neighbours' stairs would be a mirror image on the other side of the shared wall, and again put it down to them.

Until the weekend. He was helping his parents bring more bits and pieces into the house. His mother had been to the supermarket on his behalf and seemingly bought enough food for him to survive for six months. A car drew up next door, suitcases were unloaded and it was clear from the couple's conversation that this was their return from a fortnight's holiday. They said it was a shame they had not been there to welcome him to Willesden. They were a couple who lived alone.

The following night the noises came earlier, whilst Tom was still wide awake. Rebel had gone ahead of him upstairs, and as he hurried up behind, to make sure that the dog went into his own bed and not onto Tom's, he heard the same indistinguishable scraping sort of sounds coming with some regularity, seemingly from directly beneath his feet. He stopped; listened, and nothing more.

Next morning Tom bought a new washing line and a couple of galvanised dustbins with tight-fitting lids. These would do to keep Rebel's food fresh and dry. It was so much cheaper to buy it in bulk, but Tom worried about the keeping properties of the paper sacks he currently used.

It was as he made to move the dog treats into one of the bins that he noticed it, a hole in the bottom corner of the sack, through which the treats poured as he picked up and tipped the bag. The treats he called sausage rolls, though that was not their proper name. His name perfectly described the appearance of them, some sort of meaty filling, encased in a circle of crunchy biscuit. Bending down to pick up the spilt biscuits he saw that one, hard up against the skirting board, was moving. Quietly he watched, fascinated. Rebel sat beside him, with his head on one side. Slowly, almost imperceptibly, the treat was edging back into a small hole in the skirting, where the wood met the carpet. There was a tiny, tiny scratching sound if he listened carefully. The biscuit was moving so slightly Tom decided he could get on with other jobs and just check on it from time to time.

It took all day for the biscuit to disappear through the hole, which was only just big enough for it to fit. Tom could visualise it being pulled from the other side, like in a Tom and Jerry cartoon, with a tiny mouse's feet braced against the wall as he tugged and tugged. The alternative was that, having wedged the biscuit, one or more creature was eating their way through it from the other side.

Now Tom saw what had happened. One of the first jobs he had done the previous week, whilst his parents were making up his bed upstairs, was to wander out into the garden with Rebel. And then he remembered. When he had pushed over the rickety shed there had been a scurrying of tiny rodents, two adults and several baby mice. Pulling down the shed had destroyed their nest and had exposed them to the elements.

The noises he had heard from the stairs had been the mice running up the sloping floorboards that formed the ceiling of the under-stairs cupboard, but below the stair treads themselves. They had evidently been going out into the garden during the daytime and coming in at night, going upstairs and finding the stock of dog treats. They had chewed an access hole in the sack, and presumably spent hours at a time dragging these mouse-sized biscuits into the hole to feed their family of babies.

The next morning he used the old planks from the shed to construct a shelter at the far end of the garden, in a thicket of brambles that would deter Rebel from seeking them out. He blocked up the hole in the skirting board, then every couple of days he would put one of the dog treats into the shelter and within a day or so it would be gone.

He never again heard the sound of a little mouse on the stair, and Rebel, Tom and the family of little Jerrys continued to live in harmony.

Where there's a Will

I had never really considered how important it was to make a will and it took several factors to make me realise. Nor had I been aware of how difficult it was to really get to know another human being, unless they let you.

My dad had been devastated when my mum was killed in an accident. I was barely old enough to remember her, but everyone said how lovely she was, how much she loved us and so on. I haven't told you much about my dad and that's because I never felt I really knew him well. He was very hands-off. Family members wondered aloud how he was going to cope. He was an executive with one of the major airlines. A *big cheese* my aunt called him, and he travelled a lot with his job, all over the world.

Mrs Jones moved in soon after Mum died as a sort of childminder-cum-housekeeper. I never knew her true marital status, never questioned whether there was a Mr Jones anywhere around, it was just Mrs

Jones and her daughter Clarissa. Clarissa was a couple of years older than me, but went to my school so I'd seen her around. It was a big house, there was plenty of room for us all.

After a few years of living like this my dad married Mrs Jones. It didn't seem strange to me at the time. I suppose I was too young to think about it. He sat me down I remember and talked to me about principles, and morals and women's reputations being impugned, none of which I understood at the time but I've wondered since whether the neighbour's tongues had been wagging about them sharing a home.

I was fine with it to be honest, I was about eight and the woman and her daughter had been there for nearly as long as I could remember. The only changes that were evident to me was that she moved out of one of our two spare bedrooms and moved into my dad's and that I was now to call her Ella.

Dad seemed happy enough with the situation and Clarissa seemed as unaffected as I felt. Everything went swimmingly for years then when I was in my early twenties tragically my dad passed away.

It was as if a mask was ripped from Ella, revealing the true person underneath. She went off to register the death, or whatever process needs to be followed, with undue haste in my opinion. I knew more or less what was in my dad's will. He had always said that the house would be split equally between myself and Ella, with her allowed to live there for as long as she wanted. There was another proviso however, that if Ella should remarry or if a man should move into the house, it was to be immediately sold and the proceeds split between us. It seemed reasonable. As his only child I would in other circumstances have been his sole heir. He was being very honourable in all this, and it seemed very fair to me.

Thankfully his will was lodged with the family solicitors as Ella didn't quite agree that the will was fair. *Iniquitous* was just one of the things she called it. She felt that Clarissa should have been given what she called *equal billing* with myself – I know, bizarre isn't it? She also said that the clause about not moving someone into the house without forfeiting the right to live there, was intolerable.

Rightly or wrongly I was in the solicitor's office first thing the next morning. My poor father was barely dead and I felt like we fighting over his leavings like wild animals, but I felt forced to take this premature action because of Ella. The solicitor made me feel a lot better. Ella had phoned him the previous afternoon, asking about the possibility of overturning the terms of the will. Had it been properly signed? Witnessed? How could he be so sure? What about my dad's state of mind? She had been married for fourteen years, had she no rights? He told me that he had been polite but non-committal. His own office had dealt with drawing up the will, and indeed he had pointed out potential pitfalls in how my father originally wanted it wording, saying that all ambiguity must be removed. He had arranged for Ella to visit his offices the next morning so that he could go through all of this and explain it to her.

When I got home, thoroughly reassured, it was to see a strange man sitting in the kitchen. At first I took him to be from the undertakers' but then I recognised the grey jumper he was wearing. It was one I had given my father at Christmas. Excusing myself I went upstairs to my father's bedroom and flung open his wardrobe doors. As well as a few of my father's clothes – the better, newer items – there were many other garments and shoes I had not seen before. The drawers were the same, handkerchiefs, socks, underwear. In the bathroom was a strange razor, shaving foam and other male paraphernalia that had not been my dad's. I photographed it all on my phone and then telephoned the solicitor. He was surprised to hear from me so quickly and was shocked when I told him what I had found.

The following morning I was able to confirm that this man had indeed stayed overnight. Presumably Ella thought I hadn't noticed, or believed that she was still in a position to overturn my father's will. Surprisingly Clarissa, who had several years ago married and moved out, phoned to see how we were, and told me that this man had been on the scene on and off for years. It was apparently the talk of the neighbourhood that Ella was enjoying his company whilst my dad was working away.

An email arrived for me from the solicitor whilst Ella must still have been on her way to his office. The mystery man was nowhere to be seen. The solicitor had wanted to let me know before Ella told me her version, that given the terms of the will, she now had three months to move out. He would tell her that he would be asking me whether I would be gracious enough to commence that three months' notice from the day of my father's funeral, rather than immediately, and he suggested that I agreed to that when he officially asked me.

He felt it would be better for me to move out of the house also. Otherwise I would have to pay Ella her share, which she may insist upon in one lump sum or as a regular income. If the house was sold and the proceeds divided, then I could be free of Ella once and for all. I asked him about my father's other possessions, his clothes for instance, his camera and his car. He confirmed that all those things had been left to me outright.

I spent the rest of the morning clearing out my father's room. His Christmas jumper was in the wardrobe along with his other stuff. Carefully I removed everything of his, photographed every item, photographed what was left and then took all of my dad's stuff to the charity shop. On my return I called one of the car agencies that guarantee to buy any vehicle, and within a couple of hours my dad's car was sold and gone, the money deposited in my bank account.

Ella arrived back at about three o'clock. She flung the solicitor's letter on the kitchen table, 'You'd better read that.'

'I've seen it,' I told her. 'Dad's solicitor has agreed to act on my behalf, so I suggest you appoint someone else.' She looked surprised, 'for the house sale,' I told her, 'Dad's not buried yet but you were evidently keen to get on with things, so I have an estate agent coming tomorrow morning. The funeral's on Thursday next week, and three months after that you need to be gone from here.'

It was as if the reality hit her like a brick. She must have been very confident in her ability to get her own way.

'But where will I go?' she wailed.

I shrugged, 'Perhaps your friend can put you up. You'll need to return his clothes to him anyway.'

She parcelled up all the man's clothes in various bin bags, stopping every now and then to talk, presumably to him, on her phone. The last bit was the only snatch of conversation I heard. 'I'll load it in the car and bring it over.'

She had an ancient Mini that she had used for her visit to the solicitor's office. Now I saw her looking around, clearly trying to find something. 'Where are the keys to the BMW?' she asked me at last, 'There's no room for all this in the Mini.'

'Gone,' I told her. 'As I said before, you were clearly in a hurry to get on with clearing my poor father out of your life. I sold his car while you were out. If you look at the will you can see quite clearly that everything other than the house was left to me outright. If there's any of the furniture I don't need, I'll be sure to let you have first refusal. Don't help yourself, I have photographed everything. Now, I must go. I have an appointment to view a cottage later.'

If only she hadn't been so greedy. If only she hadn't been in such a rush to replace my dad. If only she had had the decency to at least bury him before she moved on, I think I would have behaved differently, but as it was … do I regret the way I acted? No, not at all.

Wordsmiths

For years Jean had religiously watched *Wordsmiths* on the television every weekday afternoon, feeling aggrieved if she missed it and had to catch up the next day. It was one of the most popular quiz programmes on television and some of the questions were satisfactorily challenging.

Vince Smith, the handsome presenter, was so quick-witted and clever. She had always thought it would be lovely to see him in real life. And now it was happening. Fleur her daughter had secured tickets and carefully explained how the day would pan out. Explained too carefully, as Jean often thought in her dealings with Fleur these days, as if she were an imbecile rather than a seventy-five year old woman. This time she was prepared to overlook the insensitivity and accept that to see a recording of Wordsmiths live would be worth any amount of family insult.

'You don't get to choose the date, you just apply for tickets and get an email to say whether you have been successful and if so, for when. We can watch three recordings that will be transmitted on sequential days, but they record all day. Our slots are the last one in the morning, starting at eleven, then the first two in the afternoon, starting at two o'clock. We'll only be able to watch the first of the afternoon ones, because Jim has to get home to go to work. You could come home with us then, or if you want to stay for the third programme you could get the tram home. Okay?' Fleur sounded anxious.

Okay? That would be fantastic. Jean was excited. She had vaguely thought for months how lovely it would be to go and see a recording of her favourite quiz programme. She loved quizzes, thrived on quizzes and regularly bought a newspaper just for the fun of having a brand new quiz or puzzle to work out. It didn't matter what it was, crosswords, code-words, Sudoku, although she liked the word-based ones best. She reckoned it helped keep her brain young, if not the rest of her. She didn't hesitate. She would have cancelled anything else to take advantage of this offer.

*   *   *

Vince Smith, the quizmaster was younger than she had thought, no more than fifty she reckoned, but just as good looking as on the television with his dark skin and mop of curly black hair. Currently he was sporting a nearly-not-there beard like Jean had seen on younger people. It was beginning to tinge with grey and it suited him. Of course she had only seen him on the television seated behind his desk, but had not expected him to be so tall. He spoke for a moment or two before the start of recording to each of the three contestants and shook their hands. Jean thought that his smile would be enough to relax her, which she supposed was the plan.

On each of the audience seats was a small notebook of about two dozen pages, along with a ballpoint pen so that they could feel involved when the quiz questions were asked. Jean sat in an end seat, with her daughter, son-in-law Jim and granddaughter Caitlin alongside her on the second row. A warm-up act passed amongst the audience explaining when they were to clap, when to cheer, when to keep quiet and that there would be an opportunity to have a go at some of the questions if none of the contestants had managed to find an answer.

During the second round none of the three contestants found the answer to one of the questions and Vince turned to the audience. Jean was amazed that she was one of only two people to put up their hand and one of the runners hurried over. The other person was seated at the back, and she guessed that of the two she was the easier to reach. The question had been an eleven-letter anagram with the clue *the writing of the lives of saints,* and the answer she had written was *hagiography,* which was correct.

'Well done,' said Vince. 'What's your name?'
Jean went very hot, 'It's Jean,' she told him as

his dark eyes bored into her face.

'Okay, Jean with-no-surname. That's very well done.'

She was so embarrassed. Not expecting him to want her surname, she slunk down in her seat. The programme continued with Jean keeping quiet until in the fourth round when another question foiled the contestants. Again Jean put up her hand, expecting lots of other people to have done the same, but no, this time she was alone.

'The city is Antwerp,' she told the same runner, who looked at Vince and shrugged. To Jean's embarrassment he unclipped his microphone and came across to her. The other staff broke off, one or two of them grabbing the opportunity to take a swig of tea while recording was paused.

'Jean, how did you get Antwerp?' he asked, 'I hadn't got that one?' He repeated the clue: '*A six-legged foolish person not able to have a cupp*a. *The answer is a city.*

Jean answered him straight away; 'An ant has six legs, a twerp is another word for a foolish person, but that gives you two T's, so you lose one cuppa and you're left with Antwerp.'

'Excellent,' he laughed, 'but I need to ask a favour of you. If an audience member does particularly well and gets more than one answer that our contestants can't get, we open ourselves up at the network to criticism and suggestions that we have plants in the audience and so on. May I ask that you exchange notes with this young lady? Is this your grand-daughter, yes? Hello Caitlin, we'll run through it again with you giving the answer exactly as Jean just did. Is that okay?' he leaned in very close and Jean noticed that his eyes were treacly brown, 'It makes better television.' So Jean handed her notes to Caitlin and the whole process was completed. When asked, Caitlin sang out her first and surnames and said, "and Jean's my nan." The audience laughed so loudly that the continuity man asked to run it again.

Jean was walking next to Jim and he turned to her as they headed for the door to break for lunch, 'He never took his eyes off you as we got ready to leave the studio, and he's watching you again now. I think you've scored a hit.'

'He is not,' Jean glanced at Vince, who was indeed smiling at her. He caught her eye and waved. She gave a little self-conscious wave in return and nearly stumbled as she caught up with the rest of the family. Vince followed the audience out, those who were leaving and said to Jean, 'That was very good. Are you coming for the two afternoon sessions, Jean?'

She explained about Jim having to be back for work after the first one, and he nodded, 'Shame.'

Later, after lunch at one of the local pubs, the ladies re-took their seats, and Jean noticed that Jim had lagged behind. The warm-up act was chatting to the audience, the runners putting out new notepads and pens, and in came the next three contestants, followed by Vince. Before taking his seat he came over to her. 'Jean. I've just spoken to your son-in-law on their way back in. He said that although the family would have to leave after the next programme is recorded, you weren't in any particular hurry. I'd love for you to stay for the third one if you would. It'd be nice to talk with you some more.

'I'll need to hang around here for about ten minutes after that, then would you allow me to take you home? Jim said it's not far from where I'm staying. It would be no trouble, in fact it would be a pleasure? My driver will be taking me that way anyway and I don't like to think of you going by tram.'

He looked so hopeful, how could she refuse? Who was she kidding? She'd have killed to have some time to chat with him on her own. Trying not to sound too needy she accepted.

* * *

'Seventy five years old and I don't think I've ever been driven by a chauffeur before,' she settled into the car beside Vince, who had changed now out of his suit into jeans and a Calvin Klein zipped top. He explained that he kept five suits at the studio and wore them in rotation for each show.

'I think of John as my driver, rather than my chauffeur, and you don't have to fish for compliments.'

'Oh, I wasn't.'

You're a very attractive lady especially when you blush. I noticed it even under the studio lights.'

Embarrassed Jean grovelled for another subject. 'Do you live in this area then?'

'No, I live in London, in Hampstead, but for six or seven months a year I'm up here for filming three days a week so I regularly stay in a small hotel. The journey's not too bad. The hotel's comfortable enough but it's not like home,'

*   *   *

The following week Jean received two complimentary tickets to watch the recording of the show, along with an invitation to lunch with Vince and the crew. He had added a handwritten note *'Please come. If you ring me on the above number I'll get John to pick you up on our way. I put two tickets in so you can bring a friend if that makes you feel more comfortable, but I hope you won't.'*

And so the friendship began.

It was three months after they had been in the audience of Wordsmiths when on three consecutive days those episodes would be transmitted. Normally Vince didn't watch himself on television, he said it was too depressing, but Jean scoffed at that and accused him in turn of fishing for compliments.

'It's a strange life isn't it? Being a household name and face must have its challenges as well as its rewards.'

'It does. Don't get me wrong I enjoy what I do but it's a lot more routine and tedious than many people think. It's very repetitive, saying the same rules of each round every time for the new contestants. A lot of time is spent in make-up,' he laughed, 'more and more time as the years pass. Oh, and the hair of course, a nightmare.' He shook his head of springy black hair, which refused to lie down no matter what he did to it. 'But when people appreciate you, it's well worth it. Letters used to come from people who are maybe house-bound and look forward to it day to day, though nowadays it's mostly on-line of course that people have their say. That makes you feel good, and then there's the other work you get because you're well known.'

'Like what?'

'Like appearances on other quizzes as a contestant. That's enjoyable and often for charity. Then there are panel shows, some intellectual and some slapstick. They're fun. It's a concern though, not so much for my generation, but for younger people coming into the business.'

'How do you mean?'

'In terms of the future. The younger audience relies on social media for entertainment a lot more than on the television. Many of them aspire to be famous, but not through quiz shows – their highlight would be an appearance on *Pairing Couples* or *I'm on the Box,* that sort of programme. By the time Caitlin's middle aged will there even be television broadcasting? The network can only continue as long as there's a viable audience. What do you think?'

Jean loved that he talked to her on this level, and treated her responses with respect. It made a nice change.

It was after they had watched the live broadcasts that Vince first stayed over. An occasional night at first, but before long he had moved all of his stuff out of the hotel and was a regular visitor whilst filming in Media City.

It wasn't long before Fleur had a word with Jean. She made sure to do it while Vince was at the studio.

Jean was brusque, 'It's really not your concern, is it? If you're worried about your inheritance you needn't be. I just have a lovely friend whose company I enjoy and who seems to feel the same about me. He says it's more homely here than an impersonal hotel. I don't see any problem.'

Then Fleur told Jean that she had phoned her sister, Jean's other daughter, in Australia. Jean laughed, 'I bet that went well.'

Fleur said nothing. Her sister had laughed at her, 'What do you expect me to do? Tell him off? Send him away? Scoot, Mr Television Man, leave my mum alone? If he did go and Mum's left on her own again, are you going step into the void, or are you expecting me to come back to England to comfort her. I'd have thought you'd be delighted, you moan enough about the prospect of maybe having to look after her when she's firm and incapable. I doubt you'd want that. You'd be as reluctant as me.'

'Okay I suppose so, but it's not right.'

'Tell me something Fleur. Would you feel the same if it had been Dad who had found himself a much younger lady friend? I bet your only concern would be that she would be a gold-digger. We know that's not the case with Vince Smith, he's a big TV personality – we've even heard of him of here in Oz. You should be glad Mum's happy and leave them alone.'

It wasn't long before Fleur tried another tack, but it was to prove as unsuccessful as the last, 'Where's Vince from?'

'London, he lives in Hampstead. Why?'

'No, I mean where was he born?' Clearly reference was being made to Vince's dark skin and hair, something Jean hadn't even considered.

'I believe he was born in the Vauxhall area, why?'

'You're being deliberately obtuse, Mum.'

Jean tried not to lose her temper, 'I'm not, my dear. You're making assumptions because Vince is exotic looking.'

Fleur didn't stay long after that.

The following week came another onslaught, 'He's a lot younger than you, isn't he?'

'Are you still on about Vince? Yes, his mother is just six months older than me.'

Vince had told her very sadly that his mother was dying, but that was private and no business of Fleur's. 'Are you being ageist now? Jean laughed to lighten the mood, but it didn't work.

'Is he interested in you for your money?' This made Jean laugh out loud, 'What money? I don't have any money?' Her daughter's mouth pursed into a line.

'Look,' Jean told her, 'Vince is a successful television personality with a lucrative career I presume. Unlike you, I haven't been insensitive enough to ask. He owns a house in Hampstead. He has a personal driver who ferries him around as well as running errands for him, and he's been staying in probably the best hotel in the area when he's filming at Media City. Why on earth would he be interested in the pension and limited savings of a widow like me? If you're worried about your inheritance, you needn't be. My will remains and will remain unchanged, although I wonder if you deserve it. Everything I have will be split fifty-fifty between you two girls. Happy now?'

Fleur didn't give up that easily, 'Mum is this wise? People are laughing at you, and at him.'

'No Fleur, you're certainly not laughing, you're embarrassed and if other people laugh I don't care, and Vince says he doesn't care either. I don't think anybody's laughing anyway, although I think some may be jealous of our friendship.'

'Jealous?' Fleur looked incredulous.

'Yes, I overheard somebody talking about my *Toy Boy*. I think they are speculating about my love life to be honest. Well, let them.'

'But … what about his reputation? He's a household name, a well-known figure off TV. He has standards to maintain.'

'Are you suggesting that by being friendly with me he's lowering his standards? Thanks a lot. Nice to know what my daughter thinks of me.'

'Oh Mum, you know I don't mean that.'

'No actually, I don't know at all that you don't mean it. I'm beginning to wonder what exactly you do mean.'

Jean counted slowly to five, then put an arm round Fleur's shoulder, 'Can't you just be happy for me? Life is good, I'm enjoying myself. Vince is enjoying life. Why can't you just get on and enjoy yours?'

'I was wondering. Is it sex?'

There was no counting to five this time, 'I am not answering that question from my own daughter. You'll have to go on wondering, and I think it's time you went.'

The damage was done, doubts had set in. That evening Jean sat in the living room next to Vince, her feet up on the sofa while they finished watching a film, 'I don't mind who knows about you staying here,' Jean began, 'but I don't want you ever to feel embarrassed in front of your friends.'

'I could never feel embarrassed, I'm proud of you. I refer to you to everyone as my very loving friend Jean. What's brought this on?'

'Oh, you know.'

'Fleur,' he was very astute. 'Fleur is not happy with the way things are going, is she? You have to see things from her point of view – it is unusual.'

Jean was indignant, 'Why? Why do I have to look at things from her point of view? Her point of view is not relevant here.'

'I think in her own way she wants the best for you. Tell me, why did you agree to me moving in here?'

Jean considered, 'I think, before I got to know you better, I really appreciated our conversations, being talked to like an adult instead of like a senile old has-been. The family tends to talk more loudly which is fair enough, my hearing isn't what it was, but also more slowly as if I'm losing my marbles. I know they mean well but it's very tiresome and very patronising.'

He laughed, 'I remember my mother when I was losing patience trying to show her something on the internet. She snapped at me: *Remember it was me that taught you how to use a spoon and how to wipe your bottom.* I've never dared talk to her like that since. You're right, it's about dignity isn't it?

'I've never asked you what you did Jean, as a career I mean.'

'I trained as a historian,' Jean told him, 'It's always something that's interested me and eventually I lectured at the university. I was fortunate to do a lot of travelling around Egypt and on the bookcase there are two reference books that I published in the nineties. I actually have a doctorate, which may account for why I don't like being talked down to.'

'You're a very clever woman. You should have applied for Wordsmiths before we got so friendly.' Jean shook her head. These days she wouldn't have the confidence.

'You couldn't really do it now anyway, people know we're such close friends, it would be deemed as a conflict of interest.'

It was just three weeks later when things began to go wrong. Jean could tell by Vince's face that all wasn't well. She poured him a drink, and waited for him to be ready to share. 'Jean there's something I think you need to be aware of.'

'Is it your mum?'

'That's one of the things I love about you. You're always thinking of someone else's problems, not your own.'

Jean frowned, 'Do I have any problems?'

'Not at the moment, but someone has been talking and the spotlight might be on you soon. Since I stopped staying at the hotel there's a chambermaid who has been talking to the press.'

He opened his laptop and showed Jean the

headline. *Toy Boy Vince Smith relaxing with his new girl friend.'* Girl was written in inverted commas and there was a blurred photograph of the two of them walking in the park.

Jean was quiet for a long time. She read the piece, the speculation, the innuendo and felt herself blush. 'I'm so sorry,' she said at last, so quietly that Vince had to strain to hear her, 'I'm an embarrassment to you.'

He took hold of her wrinkled hand, 'You're not an embarrassment to me. You are a joy to me. Members of the press are always happy to have a pop at someone in the public eye. It's what they do and how they earn their living. My mum says I look happier now than I have for years. She's right too. Forget about it, tomorrow's chip paper.'

But it didn't take long for other media outlets to pick it up and run with it. You know the sort of thing: *Has gorgeous Vince Smith got a new lady on his arm?* and *Vince Smith has cancelled his long-standing arrangement to stay in a Manchester hotel several nights a week during filming, and it is believed he may have moved in with a septuagenarian girlfriend living in the area.'*

So Jean had tried to ignore it, but it wasn't easy. She had been a follower of Vince on social media since they went to see the studio recordings, and was one of several thousands. There were the trolls of course – those with nothing to do but sit, protected by their keyboards and false names, slagging off famous people's lives because they had nothing better to do than vent their nastiness. These seemed to be mostly middle-aged women, probably with dreams of a similar relationship. The vast majority of Vince's followers weren't trolls, like Jean they were admirers. Before long they too had their vitriol to pour out, not against their idol, but against her.

Some of the social media trolls were very unkind. They accused her of having too much time on her hands and no life of her own, yet here they were, the same trolls again and again, spending this time they claimed to value so much hurling abuse at people they don't even know from behind their keyboards. She wondered whether they would dare to say the same if they met Vince face to face.

'Does it worry you?' she asked him when she had checked the headlines.

'No I'm used to it, it comes with the territory, but you didn't sign up for being followed and possibly harassed, Jean. These sort of groupies can be very unpleasant.'

'I expect I'll cope.'

And cope she did. A couple of times she was followed in the supermarket and to her daughter's house, but the press soon got bored. Vince seemed just as always, told her to ignore it, which she did. But she couldn't forget it. Always very aware of the difference in their ages it had never before seemed to matter that she was so much older, but now she felt it like a weight of responsibility.

After a few weeks everything seemed to quieten down. Even Fleur had backed off. Then one evening Vince dragged wearily into the house. Jean gave him some time after his meal, wondering if perhaps the problem was his mum. Eventually she had to speak.

'What's the matter Vince? You've been very quiet this evening.'

'Sorry, I hoped you wouldn't notice, or would just think I was tired or something.'

'You've got me worried now, what's happened?'

'A poison pen letter was sent to the Director General of the network. Saying all sorts of foul things, not naming you but very clearly naming me and making Jimmy Savile, Rolf Harris sort of noises. The DG has called a meeting for tomorrow morning, with the top brass.'

'But it's not at all the same,' Jean cried, 'those accusations were about children. I'm not a child.'

He smiled weakly, 'I know but the rumour mill grinds very fine around the media. They will dig and dig and the networks are being ultra-cautious at the moment, in the light of earlier problems. That's understandable.' He went quiet.

'What? There's something else isn't there?'

He nodded, then spoke more quietly, 'Someone has been onto the hospice where my mum is.'

'But that's horrible, it's not fair to involve her in all this. I am so sorry Vince.'

Reluctantly Jean suggested that they should stop throwing the trolls ammunition, 'You shouldn't stay here. You have to think long-term, you have your career to think of and of how upsetting this could be to your mum.'

He was shaking his head.

'It's okay to shake your head, but you have to think of your future.'

He rubbed his hand across his beard. His face was pale with dark shadows under his eyes. Today for the first time Jean thought Vince looked his age.

Eventually she took a deep breath, 'I think maybe you should move out.'

He sounded incredibly weary, and said at last, 'I will if that's what you want.'

'Of course it's not what I want Vince, but if it would be better for you ...'

He thought about it, 'When this series finishes filming next week I might go and stay at the Hampstead house for a bit. I would be nearer to Mum. She doesn't need this at the moment.'

'Of course you should, there will be a lot for you to sort out there. It will give you something to do as well as being close to the hospice. How is she anyway?' Jean was eager to change the subject from Vince's departure, but it didn't lighten the mood.

'Not great really. She's going downhill fast now. It's a horrible disease. I'll stay over in London next week if you're sure that's okay with you, to be near her?' There was a question in his voice, but Jean could tell that his mind was made up. He was distancing himself from her, but was it just because his mum was very ill? Or was it the publicity that had shaken him?

Two weeks later, with no contact made by either of them Jean found it difficult to fill her time. She was angry and upset and very, very sad. Fleur came to visit, very evidently trying not to look jubilant. 'It was always going to end in tears, Mum.'

'What tears?' Jean put mugs of tea down on the coffee table and smiled weakly at her daughter. Fleur sat in the chair she thought of as Vince's, and produced a cake out of her bag.

'I brought a cake, I thought it might cheer you up.'

Cake can't mend a broken heart Jean nearly snapped at her. 'Lovely, cake,' she managed, thinking to herself *I don't want cake, I want Vince.* The conversation spluttered on. Jean felt she must have sounded rational because it wasn't long before Fleur stood up, 'Well, I'll leave you to it.'

Leave her to what exactly Fleur didn't specify. She meant well, but Jean thought that if she heard just one more reference, however oblique, to: *I told you so* and *It was never going to work, be realistic,* she would scream. At this rate Fleur and Jim would be putting her in a home, saying she was unstable. She needed to pull herself together.

Life went on its dull, dreary way. No matter how Jean tried she wasn't able to raise her spirits. One morning she went into town and, on a whim, went into a coffee shop. She smiled at the girl who brought her coffee and opened her newspaper. There was the death notice for Marla Smith of Hampstead.

Jean's eyes blurred and the tears welled up. 'What's the matter dear,' the waitress glanced at the paper, 'Oh, somebody you know died? That's sad, I'm so sorry, dear.'

The death had taken place three days previously and the committal was scheduled for the following week at Highgate Cemetery. She decided that she would go. It would give her something to focus on and she would be able to see Vince again, if only from a distance.

She crept furtively into the back of the church, feeling like a naughty schoolgirl, and saw Vince instantly, his shock of curly hair towering over the people sitting next to him. He sat, head bowed, surrounded by elderly people. The congregation was small. Jean reckoned that Smith was such a common name, and Vince's mum had been in the hospice for so long, that many people would not have made the link.

Suddenly he turned and saw her. His face was indescribable, she could only think of love and – thankfulness was the word that came to mind. He mouthed it silently, *Thank you.* She had planned to make a hasty exit back to the station as soon as she had seen Vince and the service was over, but he was too quick for her as he hurried to her side.

'Come back to the house, Jean. Please?'

'I can't Vince, all these people. I just wanted to see you and say how sorry I am about your mum. You did your very best for her.'

'I want to see you too. I've been longing to get in touch but I wasn't sure if you'd prefer me to stay away, and then this...' He waved an arm to encompass the proceedings. 'If it worries you, none of these people know who you are. Those photographs in the newspapers are long forgotten. These are mostly family and neighbours of my mum. They don't know who you are. Please.'

Reluctantly Jean went back to the Hampstead house with Vince and the small group of people. She noticed how drawn he looked, dark bags under his eyes, shoulders bowed. She just wanted to talk to him and so she stayed on and on, just introducing herself as a friend if she was asked. If inquisitors assumed she meant a friend of his mum rather than of Vince, she didn't put them right. After what seemed an age, the last mourner went home and Vince breathed out wearily.

'Are you sleeping? You look so tired,' Jean was solicitous.

'Not really. In fact,' he looked squarely at her, 'hardly at all since I last saw you. I've missed you so much.'

'Come back.' she said spontaneously, then immediately retracted it, 'I'm sorry, that was wrong of me. You're hurting and it's not fair to take advantage of your vulnerability.'

He stood in front of her and took each of her hands in his. 'Please, do take advantage of it. I'd love to go back to how we were before all that unfair publicity. Do you think we ever could?'

Jean looked at him very seriously. 'The only problem I can see …

He grimaced, 'I know, Fleur's reaction.'

She turned her face up to him, 'To be honest I hadn't given a thought to Fleur. I was thinking that if I drove up when you next go up to Manchester I'll waste my return rail ticket.'

'No you weren't. You were worried about this all kicking off again, but I've given it a lot of thought Jean. I haven't been in touch because I wasn't sure whether you wanted me to, but now I know. We've been concerned about people we don't know and who have insignificant little lives. Let's not be martyrs to a cause that exists only in their small minds, that way we let them hijack our happiness and dictate the terms of our lives. Travel in comfort with me. If we are seen together I don't care, I'm proud to be seen with you and we'll face any fallout together. I would love to share your company.'

How could she refuse? And why should she? By the end of the week they were once again ensconced in her little house with the fire lit, gazing into the flames. He was looking more relaxed. She asked him: 'Why?'

He leaned over and smoothed her grey hair, then took her hands, wrinkled and dappled with liver spots.

'Why what? Why am I here? Why am I so much happier than I was a few weeks ago? Because you're lovely, and a wonderful, relaxing, intelligent person to spend my time with. You don't make demands, you have your own fulfilling life so you aren't over-dependent. I always look forward to being with you and when we are together I feel surrounded by a warm glow. Isn't that enough?'

And do you know? For Jean it definitely was.

Acknowledgements

I firstly need to acknowledge the contribution of my daughter, whose interest in British Sign Language triggered the writing of this book.

Her interest was mirrored and built upon by her daughter Grace Parker, who became interested to the extent of making BSL her future career and who is currently studying BSL at one of just four UK universities offering this as an undergraduate subject.

I want to thank members of the book club, Clare, Freda, Gayle, Gill, Hilary, Julie, Kerry, Liz, Steph, Sue B and Sue R Steph, who have tolerated being read to and who have commented, informing changes to some of the stories.

Many thanks to Bowen's Book Publicity for wonderful promotional posts.

Lastly I want to thank Beryl and Roy Howitt for the idea for the story *Grandad Tick Tock.*

If you have enjoyed reading this and other books by Alison Lingwood, please leave feedback on amazon.co.uk

Printed in Great Britain
by Amazon

78990845R00112